MAKING IT

It's back to square one for C.C., Robin, Gail and Annette, members of *Overnight Sensation*. It's not long since they were the talk of the music press, the latest band to hit the news, but that seems like years ago. They had a manager, then, but now they're on their own. They haven't been in the music business long but they know enough about it to realize that there are a lot of people out there ready to take advantage – their manager was one of them.

Now it's just the four of them. They've got a lot of work to do but they are determined to succeed. Everything seems to be happening at once and it's not all easy. They're not just setting up a band by themselves and trying to cut a demo tape to clinch a record deal, they've also got to find enough money to live on, let alone pay for studio time, and they're leaving home – and then there's those new romances . . .

Right now they've got millions of things to sort out, but just one thing to aim for – they want to be rock stars!

Fran Lantz is a former rock musician, children's librarian and nanny. She lives in Brookline, Massachusetts, with her husband, three guitars, and a large rock 'n' roll record collection.

+ *Plus* ▶

Another book by Fran Lantz

CAN'T STOP US NOW

FRAN LANTZ

Making It On Our Own

PENGUIN BOOKS

PENGUIN BOOKS

Published by the Penguin Group
27 Wrights Lane, London W8 5TZ, England
Viking Penguin Inc., 40 West 23rd Street, New York, New York 10010, USA
Penguin Books Australia Ltd, Ringwood, Victoria, Australia
Penguin Books Canada Ltd, 2801 John Street, Markham, Ontario, Canada L3R 1B4
Penguin Books (NZ) Ltd, 182–190 Wairau Road, Auckland 10, New Zealand

Penguin Books Ltd, Registered Offices: Harmondsworth, Middlesex, England

First published in the USA by Dell Publishing Co., Inc. 1986
Published in Penguin Books 1988

Printed and bound in Great Britain by
Cox & Wyman Ltd, Reading

For Frank Griswold,
whose humor and good sense helped
me to emerge from adolescence
relatively unscathed

1

Robin Quinn turned up the volume on her electric guitar and hammered out a series of high-powered seventh chords. Behind her Annette Giraldi pounded out the rhythm on her drum set and chomped her bubblegum in time to the bass-drum beat. A second later Gail Harrison came in on the piano, adding funky embellishments over Robin's guitar. Now C. C. Collins stepped up to the microphone. Tossing her long blond hair over her shoulder, she gazed out at the darkened high school auditorium and started to sing,

> *"Well, I may be crazy, but I've got this dream,*
> *I'm gonna make the whole world stand up and*
> *   scream.*
> *I gotta find me a place where I belong,*
> *So don't try to hold me down, cuz I'll be gone,*
> *   gone, gone."*

The whole band joined in on the chorus. "You can't stop me now! No, baby, you can't stop me now!"

C.C. was starting in on the second verse when suddenly her microphone let out a high-pitched squeal that made everyone cringe. "Ouch!" she cried, jumping back. "What's going on?"

"Feedback," Robin said wearily. "This PA system was designed for school assemblies, not rock 'n' roll."

"Look, let's take a break," Annette suggested. She

put down her drumsticks and pushed her short black hair out of her eyes.

"Good," Robin replied, taking off her guitar and leaning it against her amp. "I have something to tell you."

Gail, C.C., and Annette jumped off the stage and sat in the first row of chairs, but Robin held back a minute, watching them. Boy, she thought happily, it's great to be together again, playing music *our* way, without Reg here to boss us around.

Reg Barthwaite. What a mess he'd made of their lives. Oh, sure, his plan had sounded good at first. All they had to do was listen to him and they'd be famous —a record contract, a television show, the whole bit. "I see you girls as a sort of junior version of the Go-Go's," he'd told them. But what he really had in mind was more like a cross between the Monkees and the Dallas Cowboys Cheerleaders. Four cute little teenagers in matching cheerleader costumes, churning out wimpy sixties songs while they wiggled their hips and smiled. C.C. and the Seniors, he'd called them. Man, thought Robin, even the name was dumb!

But all that's over now, she reminded herself. She thought back to the group's big debut at the Supermarket, and her heart beat a little faster just remembering what she'd done. Instead of playing the drippy songs Reg had selected, she'd led the band through "You Can't Stop Me Now" and a bunch of other originals. The audience had loved it. But not Reg. So they quit, temporarily broke up, then re-formed as Overnight Sensation. Great! Only problem was that without Reg behind them, they had practically no instruments, no money, and only a high school auditorium to practice in. Oh, yeah, and no record contract either.

"Hey," called Annette, "what are you waiting for, a formal invitation?"

"I thought you had something to tell us," C.C. added. She flicked a piece of lint off her skintight black leather pants. "So what is it?"

"It must be bad," Gail said, nervously running her hand through her short-cropped Afro. "Otherwise she would have told us right away."

"All right, already. Relax." Robin sat down on the edge of the stage. "I have some good news and some bad news," she told them.

"What is this?" C.C. asked. "A comedy routine?"

Robin shot her a withering look. "First the bad news. Remember those record-company guys who called me after we dumped Reg?"

"Sure," Annette replied. "They were real interested in us. Too bad we'd just broken up."

"Right. Well, now that we're together again, I figured they might still be interested."

C.C. leaned forward. "And . . . ?"

Robin shook her head. "Forget it. The guy at RCA didn't even remember who I was. When I reminded him, he said, 'Oh, that's yesterday's news.' The guy at Epic remembered me, but he told me he'd just signed another all-girl band and the label didn't want to promote more than one."

"Those morons!" Annette muttered.

"Forget 'em," said C.C., lighting a cigarette. "They're jerks."

"Maybe so," replied Robin, "but they're the people with the power. Anyhow, here's the good news. I talked to one nice guy. His name is Ben Kaplan and he works at Backstage Records. He actually said what the other guys had only implied—that record companies were interested in us mostly because we were making news, not because they thought our music was so great."

"That's good news?" Gail asked skeptically.

Robin smiled. "No, but this is. Ben *does* like our music. In fact, he told me he thinks we have real promise. He said if we make a demo tape he'll definitely give it his consideration."

"A demo tape?" Annette repeated. "Won't that cost money?"

"It sure will," C.C. told her. She pointed her finger at Robin. "Listen, if this guy isn't offering a contract, then forget it. We'll go somewhere else."

Robin eyed C.C. with disdain. "Like where, for instance?"

"Anywhere. Reg told us he had dozens of record companies interested in us. Television producers too. Just call them up."

Robin sighed. "Look, I don't think you understand. Some groups record dozens of demo tapes—not to mention singles and albums—before they ever get signed to a label. In fact, most groups never get signed at all."

"But Reg said—"

"Look," Robin snapped, "Reg isn't our manager anymore."

"Hey," said Annette, "relax. You don't have to yell at us, you know."

Robin sighed. "I'm sorry. But what did you expect? You act as if all we had to do was get the band back together and wait for the offers to roll in."

"I'm not *that* naive," C.C. said resentfully, dropping her cigarette butt into an empty Diet Coke can. "But still . . ."

"I don't know *what* I thought," Annette said honestly. "When Reg was our manager, things just seemed to *happen.*"

"That's right," agreed Robin, pushing her brown curls out of her eyes. "But things are different now. We have to convince the record companies that we're worth signing. No one's going to do it for us." She crossed her long legs and looked at the girls. "Unless, of course, we don't want to be famous. I mean, we could just play together for the fun of it, if that's all you're interested in. No one's forcing us to make a tape. We don't even have to perform anywhere, if we don't want to."

"Are you kidding?" C.C. asked incredulously. "Do you think I walked out on Reg so I could go back to being a normal American teenager? Fat chance! I want to be a star!"

"Me too!" Annette chimed in.

"Right," agreed Gail. "I wouldn't have put my classical music career on hold if I wasn't serious about this band. I want us to succeed."

"Okay," Robin said eagerly. "Then listen. The first thing we need to do is raise some money. The only equipment we have is an electric guitar, a drum set, and a couple of amps. We need a bass, an electric piano, mikes—the list is practically endless. We need a decent practice space, too, but for the time being I guess we'll have to keep practicing here. Then when we get enough money to buy decent equipment, we can really get down to the serious stuff, like recording a demo tape and playing around town."

"And how do you propose we raise this money?" C.C. asked. "Rob a bank?"

"Not quite. I figure we'll have to get part-time jobs."

Moans of dismay echoed through the auditorium. "My parents have been bugging me for months to get a job," Annette whined. "If I give in, they'll force me to put my whole salary away for college tuition."

"My father doesn't want any of us to work until we have to," Gail said with a worried frown. "He said he had to start working when he was sixteen and he wants it to be different for us."

C.C. contorted her shapely lips into a pout. "Well, my mother told me that if I got a job, my father would stop paying child support and we'd have to sell our house." She shook her head. "Besides, all my spare time is reserved for Kurt."

"You must get a pretty big allowance, don't you?" Robin asked, carefully steering the conversation away from boys. She didn't want to be reminded that C.C. was the only member of Overnight Sensation who had a boyfriend. Annette claimed boys just held you down, and Gail still had a crush on her old piano teacher, but Robin was definitely in the market for a guy. If only she could find someone who liked her *and* rock 'n' roll . . .

"My allowance isn't *that* big," C.C. was saying. "Besides, I have to use it to buy makeup and clothes. And don't tell me that's being selfish either. I'm the lead singer in this group, and if I don't look good, we won't get anywhere."

Robin raised her eyes heavenward and let out an exasperated sigh. "Listen, I don't want to work, either, but where else are we going to get the money? A bass guitar alone costs over a hundred dollars, and that's for a really crummy one."

Gail nodded sheepishly. "You're right," she conceded. "Maybe I can find a job my parents will approve of." She paused thoughtfully. "My brother knows someone who plays the piano at ballet rehearsals. I'll ask him about it."

Annette shrugged. "I guess I just won't tell my parents. If they don't know I have a job, they can't make me put away the money."

Robin grinned. "Great. Now, what about you, C.C.?"

"Okay, okay," she said irritably. "Relax. I'll come up with something."

Robin swung her leg over the edge of the stage. "I just wish it was June and we were all out of school. Then we'd have a lot more time to devote to the band."

"The first thing we better devote ourselves to is finding a place to practice," Annette said glumly. "After I graduate, we won't be able to rehearse here anymore."

Robin had a faraway look in her eyes. "If only we could find a loft in the Village or down in SoHo. . . ."

"Wouldn't that be awfully expensive?" Gail asked.

"Not if we lived there too. We could share all the expenses and the chores. We could partition off the corners for bedrooms and set up our instruments in the middle. Whenever we wanted to practice, we'd just sit down and play."

"Hey," said Annette, "I didn't know you were planning to move out. I thought you got along great with your family."

"I do—most of the time, anyway. But I can't practice in our apartment. Every time I turn the amplifier up above a whisper, the old lady downstairs freaks out. Besides," she added with a shrug, "living at home is okay when you're in high school, but I'm a college freshman now. I want to get out on my own."

"Me too," Annette agreed eagerly. "And if we all found a place together—"

"Do you really think the four of us could live together?" C.C. scoffed. "We'd be at each other's throats in five minutes!"

"No, we wouldn't," Gail told her. "Whenever we felt like yelling at each other, we could just pick up our instruments and start playing. We'd get all our aggression out through our music."

"Right," laughed Robin. Jumping up she grabbed

her guitar and tore into a searing rock 'n' roll riff. Throwing back her head like a television evangelist she cried, "Children, I'm not angry anymore. I've been saved by the power of rock 'n' roll!"

The girls erupted with laughter. "Hey"—Annette grinned—"I could use a little salvation right now. Let's play some more music."

"All *right!*" Robin exclaimed. "I've even got a new song to teach you." The girls ran back onstage and picked up their instruments. "Okay," she said eagerly. "I think you're gonna like this one. It's a real rocker." She hit a blazing power chord and started to sing.

> *"It's time to shake up the status quo,*
> *Knock down the old boss, take control,*
> *Gonna teach this town how to rock 'n' roll,*
> *Come on, girls, now, here we go!"*

Strumming her guitar Robin danced across the stage while the other girls clapped along. "No time to stop, no hesitation!" she wailed. "We're gonna be an overnight sensation!"

Annette picked up the beat, Gail tried out a few experimental chords on the piano, and by the end of the second chorus they were all playing together. Robin shook her head in amazement. All I have to do is sing a new song once and they've got it. Man, this band is great! She nodded thoughtfully. Now, if we can just convince the rest of the world . . .

When the next chorus came around, the whole band joined in. "We're gonna be an overnight sensation!" they cried, jumping up and down in time to the beat.

Robin threw her head back and tossed off a burning riff on her guitar. "Look out, world!" she shouted into the empty auditorium. "We're Overnight Sensation and we're ready to rock. All the way to the top!"

||||||||||||||||||||||| **2**

C.C. was leaning against a stop light on the corner of Fifth Avenue and Thirty-fourth Street, waiting for her boyfriend and thinking about the band. We're sounding better and better all the time, she thought with satisfaction. In fact, I'll bet once the record companies hear our demo tape they'll be falling all over themselves to sign us up. Only problem is, we need money to make the tape. . . .

C.C. tried to imagine herself working at some part-time job. What kind of jobs did teenagers get, anyway? Waitress? Sales clerk? Baby-sitter? No, there had to be an easier way to get her hands on some money. She'd ask her mother to increase her allowance, and if that didn't work—

"Hey, little lady! Lookin' for a good time in the big city?"

Startled, C.C. looked up. A black Fiat sports car was pulling up to the curb. Before she could decide what to do about it, her boyfriend, Kurt Vandenburg, stuck his head out the car window and grinned.

"Oh, Kurt," C.C. scolded, "you scared me!"

He laughed. "Didn't recognize the car, huh? It's my dad's. Come on. Get in before you freeze."

C.C. opened the car door and slid in next to Kurt. Without a word he pulled her close and kissed her.

Her lips, cooled by the January winds, melted into his, and suddenly she wasn't cold anymore.

"Why did you want me to meet you here?" Kurt asked. "I could have picked you up in Short Hills."

"Are you kidding? My mother would freak if she saw me dressed like this!" She opened her coat to reveal a red-and-gold-striped Danskin jump-suit with a studded black leather belt, black boots, and black fingerless gloves.

"I see what you mean." He chuckled, pulling out into the midtown Manhattan traffic. "But you look great to me."

Glowing with pleasure C.C. sat back in the seat and looked at Kurt. Once she had thought his cute face—short, dark-brown hair, brown eyes with long eyelashes, delicate upturned nose—didn't look mature enough to be interesting. But that was back in the days when she was crazy over the band's manager, Reg Barthwaite. C.C. shook her head. These days it was hard to remember what she'd seen in Reg. Oh, sure, he was older—thirty, at least—and handsome, sort of like Sting in the Police. But he was a creep, too, she reminded herself. The only thing he wanted out of me was sex—that, and using me to convince the rest of the band to do things his way.

"C.C., are you listening to me? You look like you're off in outer space."

"Oh, Kurt, I'm sorry. It's nothing." She had never told him about her relationship with Reg, and she didn't want to. It made her feel like a jerk to realize she'd fallen for Reg so easily. "What were you saying?" she asked.

"I said we're going to Touch. It's one of those new art clubs downtown. They have all kinds of cool stuff going on—music, fashion shows, comedy, art exhibits . . ."

"Sounds great!" She stretched out her legs and added, "Boy, it feels great to get out of New Jersey. When I'm in Manhattan, everything seems to look up. You know what I mean?"

Kurt shrugged. "We've been through this before. The city is exciting, no doubt about that. If I'm ever going to make it as an artist, this is the place to be. Still, I kind of like Short Hills."

"But all those horse shows and debutante balls and cocktail parties are such crap. It's just showing off. Who needs it?"

"Me, I guess. I mean, that's the way I was raised. It just seems natural to me."

C.C. nodded thoughtfully. "That's where we're different, I guess. Your family's always had money. We were pretty middle class until my father started his investment firm." She rolled her eyes. "He makes a killing in wheat groats or hog bellies or something, and next thing I know my parents are falling all over themselves to make it onto the society page. Maybe that's what they want," she added with a shake of her head, "but it's not for me."

"Hey, for someone who hates that kind of thing, you seemed to be having a pretty good time at your coming-out party. Or were you just faking it to make me feel good?"

"That was different," she replied, smiling self-consciously. "I always have a good time when I'm with you." She pictured herself in Kurt's arms, gliding across the dance floor. The memory made her stomach flutter with pleasure.

Kurt smiled, then paused and asked seriously, "How are things going at home?"

The pleasant feeling in C.C.'s stomach disappeared as her muscles contracted into a tense knot. It was always that way when she thought about her parents' divorce. "I don't know," she began uncertainly. "Mother's still drinking. It's only been a couple weeks since Daddy filed for divorce, but . . . well, I didn't think it would be this bad." She shrugged. "At least she knows how to handle it. No passing out or throwing up or embarrassing herself in public. That, as she would put it, just wouldn't do. I'm the only one who sees it, really. Like when she comes home giggling and then turns around and starts crying. And the next morning, watch out! She's a bitch when she has a hangover."

"Poor C.C. Have you told your father?"

"No. I haven't seen him since my coming-out party. Besides, if I told him and my mother found out . . . Oh, I don't know. Maybe I should call him."

Kurt reached over and gently ran his hand over her hair. "Don't think about it now," he said softly. "Tonight we're going to get away from all that and just have fun."

"Sounds wonderful," C.C. said with a determined nod. She reached over and flipped on the radio. "I'm ready to rock!"

While David Bowie sang about modern love, Kurt drove through Chinatown and parked down by the docks on the East River. Hand in hand they walked down the street until they came to a dilapidated brick warehouse. A picture of a dancing couple had been painted on the door and the word TOUCH seemed to be exploding out of their mouths.

Kurt opened the door and they walked inside. They were in a cavernous room with black walls and a high ceiling. Large pieces of sculpture were spread out across the floor, along with a few picnic tables and wooden benches. Some people were dancing to the pounding synthesized music, some were drinking at the picnic tables, and some were wandering around, looking at the art.

"What do you think?" Kurt yelled over the music. "Pretty far out, huh?"

"I love it!"

"Great. Let's dance."

C.C. and Kurt joined the crowd and started shaking to the beat. It wasn't quite as nice as gliding across a ballroom in Kurt's arms, she decided, but at least the music was hipper than the big band standards they'd danced to at her coming-out party. As she moved, she looked around at the sculptures. A huge Fiberglas hand, a naked mannequin strung with Christmas lights, a stack of dented garbage cans . . . Pretty wild! She looked back at Kurt and smiled. He wasn't dressed as flamboyantly as some of the other people—just jeans, a black shirt, and a pink tie—and he didn't exactly dance so much as sway from side to side. But to C.C he was the most interesting, most attractive, most exciting person in the place.

"Come on," Kurt said, after a few minutes. "I have a surprise for you."

"What?" she asked eagerly, wiping the beads of perspiration from her forehead.

He led her across the room to one of the artworks—a tentlike enclosure made with trees branches, pipes, and pieces of multicolored fabric. "Go inside," he told her.

Hesitantly C.C. lowered her head and half walked, half crawled, into the tent. A light bulb hung from the ceiling, dimly illuminating a small table. On the table were some dried flowers, a black leather glove, some Monopoly money, a record album by the Cool, a white high heel, and an open book. C.C. leaned over to look more closely. It was *Amy Vanderbilt's Complete Book of Etiquette,* and it was opened to the section on debutante balls.

Fascinated, C.C. stared at the table. Every one of the objects on it held some special significance for her. The record—well, Reg Barthwaite had produced the Cool's first album. That white high heel—why, it looked just like the one she had worn to her deb ball. And that black leather glove—she'd lost one just like it on her last date with Kurt. . . .

Backing out of the tent C.C. turned to him with a quizzical smile on her face. "W-What is that?" she stammered. "Is it . . . I mean, did you . . . ?"

Kurt nodded. "Yes, I made it. It's called *Portrait of C.C.* You see, I wanted to create a piece of art that would express who you are. Not just a drawing of your face—a camera could do that—but something that really captures your spirit. I wanted to show the two sides of C.C.—the proper young debutante your parents want you to be, and the rock 'n' roll woman you really are." Thrusting his hands into his pockets he shrugged and laughed nervously. "Well, what do you think?"

C.C. shook her head with amazement and delight. "Kurt, you're incredible! I mean, when I walked in there I thought, This place is like . . . like, it's *me.*" Smiling radiantly, she threw her arms around Kurt and hugged him. "I love it!"

"Whew! I'm really glad. If you hadn't liked it, I don't know what I would have done. Maybe tear it down and go to law school like my parents want me to."

"No way! You're an artist. But how did you get it in here?"

"Well, I've been taking my portfolio around to all the galleries. None of the uptown places were interested, but when I came here they asked to see slides of my latest work. I showed them some and told them my idea for *Portrait of C.C.,* and they said, 'Okay, go ahead.' " He smiled shyly. "I was so excited. I was going to run right home and tell you, but then I thought, What if she doesn't like it? Finally I decided to wait till it was done and just surprise you." He pointed to the tent. "See that cloth I used? It's got hearts all over it." She nodded. "Well, that's supposed to represent something too." His voice grew softer, until it was almost a whisper. "It's my love, C.C., surrounding you, protecting you. . . ."

C.C.'s heart leapt into her throat. "Oh, Kurt, I . . ." But she didn't have to say anything else because he took her in his arms and kissed her.

"I have another surprise," he whispered, still hugging her. He cleared his throat. "Um, let's sit down."

Puzzled, C.C. followed Kurt to an empty picnic table and took a seat. Some sort of fashion show was going on in the middle of the room. Male models, dressed entirely in white, were parading around to the Billy Idol song "White Wedding." Turning her back on the scene she looked at Kurt. "What is it?" she asked.

"This morning my dad told me he's going on a business trip," he began, taking her hand. "To London and Paris. He'll be gone a month, maybe longer."

"Yeah, so?" C.C. wasn't sure why, but her stomach was beginning to churn.

"So," Kurt continued, "he asked me to come along. At first I said no way. I mean, I know I promised my dad I'd put off college for a year and work at his office, but I had no idea how much I'd hate it." He paused and looked down at the floor. "But then I thought, Hey, we're talking London and Paris here. I could go to the Louvre, the British Museum, maybe even travel around a little on my own. The more I thought about it, the more I was sure I'd be a fool to say no." He squeezed her hand. "So . . . so I'm going."

C.C. felt tears welling up into her eyes. It was ridiculous, she knew, but she couldn't help it. She hadn't known Kurt very long—only a couple of months, really—but she cared for him more than she had ever thought she could care for anybody. Since her coming-out party they'd spent practically all their time together, and C.C. knew that without Kurt to lean on it would have been a lot harder to deal with her parents' divorce.

But now he was going away. A month, maybe longer. And what if he really liked it over there? What if he told his dad he wanted to spend the year traveling all over Europe? Why, he might even decide he wanted to go to art school over there.

C.C. gazed up into Kurt's face. He looked so eager, so wide-eyed and hopeful. What does he expect me to say? she asked herself. *Go on. Have a great time. Maybe you'll meet some nice French girl. I don't mind.* Is that what he wants? The thought made her furious. Forget it, she fumed. If he wants to go off and leave me, that's fine, but he'd just better realize I'm not going to lock myself in my room until he gets back.

"C.C. . . . ?"

"Have a good time," she said coolly.

"Oh, C.C., I know you're upset. I am too. I really agonized over this. I don't want to leave you, but—"

"Hey, relax. Everything's cool. This is a free country, right?" She shrugged. "You do what you want, I'll do what I want, and we'll see where we stand when you get back."

Kurt squeezed her hand. "But, C.C., nothing has to change. It's just a month, and then we'll be back together."

"No promises," she insisted. "I'd rather just play it by ear."

Kurt pulled his hand away, and C.C. thought he looked a little relieved. "Well, okay," he said, "if that's the way you want it . . ."

"I do," she replied, turning back to the center of the room. The fashion show had ended and some sort of campy comedy show was going on. A group of people dressed as Boy George were singing "I Enjoy Being a Girl." It didn't seem funny to C.C., but she threw back her head and laughed anyway.

I've been hurt by guys before, she reminded herself. Daddy walked out, and Reg played me for a fool. But no more. I'm too smart to let that happen again. Besides, when the band gets famous I'll have all the boys I want. One for every night of the week. She wiped a tear from the corner of her eye and forced herself to smile. Kurt can jump off the Eiffel Tower, for all I care, she thought with satisfaction. I'm going to spend the next month having fun.

 3

Robin stepped inside the Top of the Pops Record Shop and looked around. Bins of records lined the narrow aisles, and the walls and ceiling were covered with rock posters, T-shirts, and buttons. Outside, rain beat against the windows, providing background sound ef-

fects to the song that was playing on the stereo—
"Rain," by the Beatles.

Robin's brown hair hung in damp curls across her
forehead and against her cheeks. Unwinding her scarf
from her neck she used it to wipe the rain from her
face. The middle-aged man behind the counter looked
up. Robin made eye contact and smiled her cheeriest
smile. "Hi," she said. "Nice weather, huh?"

"Mmm. Help you?" he asked in a bored voice.

"I hope so. I'm looking for a part-time job. Do you
know if there's anything available?"

The man snorted a laugh and turned to face her. "I
just laid off my Sunday help. It was cheaper to close
the store than pay another salary." He shrugged. "I
can't compete with the chains. If it wasn't for the local
singles and small labels I stock, I'd be out of business."

Robin nodded glumly. "Well, I'll just leave my
name and number in case things pick up." She handed
him one of the slips of paper she'd filled out at home.
"Thanks."

Robin looked out the door. The rain was still heavy
and the wind was grabbing unsuspecting umbrellas
and dragging them off down the street. Reluctant to
leave the warm, dry store she strolled down the center
aisle and glanced through the bins.

But for a change Robin's mind wasn't on music.
She'd spent the last week visiting every record store
and music shop from midtown to TriBeCa, trying to
find a job. Everywhere the answer was the same. "I
don't hire part-timers . . . try again in June . . .
sorry, I just hired someone. . . ." In other words, forget it.

Obviously, the answer was to look for something
less interesting but more realistic, the kind of job that
teenagers could get without too much trouble. But the

idea of scooping ice cream or waiting on tables left her cold, and she was damned if she was going to put on one of those ugly little uniforms they made you wear at McDonald's and Burger King.

Oh, well, she reminded herself, Chrissie Hynde worked as a waitress before she left Akron, Ohio, and even Elvis Presley started out as a truck driver. Turning from the bins Robin walked up the aisle toward the front of the store. The rain had decreased to a steady drizzle, so she threw her damp scarf around her neck and prepared to leave.

That was when she noticed the pile of *Rock Rag* magazines next to the door. Stopping in her tracks Robin grabbed an issue and turned to the man behind the counter. "How much?"

"Look at the cover," he said wearily. "They're free. God forbid you should have to buy anything."

Ignoring the sarcasm Robin took the issue and left. Out on the street she stopped under an awning and flipped eagerly through the magazine, looking for his name. There it was, at the top of an article about the country punk craze. Ian Harkin! Robin's heart beat a little faster just looking at it.

Robin had met Ian the night Overnight Sensation (or C.C. and the Seniors, as they were known back then) performed at the Supermarket. He had run after her as she was leaving the building with Annette and Gail. "I'm writing about the concert for *Rock Rag*," he'd told her. "It's a new magazine that covers the music scene in lower Manhattan."

Robin could still see Ian's lanky body, his high cheekbones and dark eyes. From the first glance she'd thought he was handsome. His personality, however, was another matter. Ian seemed to think he was a big deal just because he'd produced a couple of demo tapes for some obscure local bands. Even more infuriating, he'd had the nerve to tell Robin she'd be a pretty good songwriter "in a year or two." *Conceited,* Robin had decided that night.

But that was over a month ago, and since then Robin had often found herself thinking about Ian's smile and the way it lit up his slender face. She'd seen him one more time, at the concert C.C. had arranged when the band got back together, and she liked him even better then. He still seemed a little cocky, but he'd been nice enough to lend the band some of his equipment, so obviously he couldn't be all bad.

Now, reading over Ian's article in *Rock Rag,* Robin had an idea. Maybe, just *maybe,* she could get a job working there. After all, the first issue of *Rock Rag* she'd seen had been only four pages long. This issue was sixteen pages, with lots of ads. They must be doing pretty well. Even if they didn't need writers, maybe she could do something else—typing or printing, or whatever it was you did with magazines. And if she happened to end up spending some time with Ian, well, that would be okay too.

Eagerly Robin scanned the magazine's masthead, searching for an address. The offices were on Avenue B in the heart of the East Village. Not exactly a classy neighborhood, Robin thought uncomfortably. Still, anything is better than serving up boxes of Chicken McNuggets. Thrusting her copy of *Rock Rag* under her arm she turned up her collar and headed across town in the direction of the East Village.

Robin was a native New Yorker with a pretty good grasp of Manhattan's neighborhoods, but Avenue B, she had to admit, was hard to characterize. Walking north toward Eleventh Street she saw punks with spiky hair, bums in filthy overcoats, elderly men and women speaking some unidentifiable Eastern European language, and young mothers pushing baby strollers. Half the buildings were deserted and deteriorating, but there was a crowded restaurant on the corner called Life, and a Celtic bookstore across the street. A mural of giant snakes in Day-Glo green and orange covered the façade of one boarded-up building. Next to that was the headquarters of a motorcycle club called the Newcomers. Three shiny Harley-Davidsons were parked outside.

The dilapidated brick building that supposedly housed the editorial offices of *Rock Rag* was about halfway up the block. Like the rest of the street it was in a state of disrepair. The windows on the top three floors were boarded over and the steps leading up to the front door were covered with old newspapers and empty beer bottles.

Can this really be the place? Robin wondered, gingerly making her way up the stairs and peering at the five buzzers on the wall by the door. Sure enough, a small hand-lettered sticker above the first buzzer said *Rock Rag,* FIRST FLOOR. KNOCK OR THROW SOMETHING AT THE WINDOW. Hesitantly she tried an experimental knock. "Yeah?" someone called from inside.

"Hello!" Robin yelled at the door, feeling a little foolish. "Uh, can I come in?"

No one answered, but a moment later the door opened and she found herself looking up at a teenager in a red beret and red mirrored sunglasses. "Hi," he drawled in a soft southern accent. "What can I do for ya?"

"Uh, is the editor of *Rock Rag* around?"

"Sure, come on in." Robin followed the boy through a small, dingy foyer and into a large, equally dingy room. The room was mostly empty except for three or four long tables covered with piles of papers, magazines, pencils, and one old manual typewriter. The walls were blank except for the peeling paint and a large poster advertising an old CBGB's concert featuring Blondie and Talking Heads.

The only person in the room was sitting at the typewriter with his back to Robin, slowly pecking away at the keys. "Hey, Ian," announced the kid in the beret. "Someone here to see you."

Ian stopped typing and stood up. When he saw Robin, his eyes widened with surprise. Then, slowly, his long face broke into a grin. "Well, hi, there," he said cheerfully, walking across the room to meet her. "How's it goin'?"

Robin felt weak all over. Ian looked even more handsome than she'd remembered. She loved his haircut—short on the sides, but curly on top, with one perfect ringlet that hung down over his forehead. His gray parachute pants hung loosely on his slender frame and his faded Hard Rock Cafe T-shirt was cut so short it revealed a few light-brown hairs on his flat stomach.

Frantically Robin tried to remember what she was wearing. With a sinking heart she realized she had dressed conservatively for her job hunt. Why didn't I wear something hipper? she moaned silently, looking down at her boring tan overcoat and gray wool slacks. Then, suddenly, Robin realized that Ian was waiting for her to say something. Blurting out the first thing that came to her mind she said, "I didn't know *you* were the editor of *Rock Rag.*"

"I am now," he replied with a chuckle. "The guy who started the magazine backed out, and for some crazy reason I decided to take over. We've only put out three issues so far, and as you can see, we're not exactly rolling in money."

"Yeah," muttered Robin, wishing her wet hair

weren't dripping down her back. She considered taking off her coat, but changed her mind when she remembered she was wearing a nerdy "Dress For Success" blouse with a bow in the front.

"How's the band?" he asked. "Thinking about cutting a demo tape yet?"

Ian's question reminded Robin of the night they'd met at the Supermarket. "When you're ready to make a tape, I might be interested," he'd told her, tossing off the remark as if he were doing her a big favor.

Robin frowned. He thinks he's so cool, she thought irritably. Well, I'll show him. Instead of telling the truth she shrugged casually and said, "We don't have to make a demo. Ben Kaplan over at Backstage Records is real interested in the band. We're waiting to see what kind of deal he offers. If it's not good enough, we'll talk to Warner Bros. or RCA."

Ian lifted his eyebrows and nodded appreciatively. "Not bad." He smiled and added, "When you're rich and famous, just remember who predicted it first."

How could she forget? She had Ian's review of the Supermarket gig taped to the wall of her bedroom. "If she keeps improving," he'd written, "there's no doubt in my mind that Robin Quinn will someday be a star."

Suddenly Robin felt sorry she'd lied. She wished she could tell Ian the truth—that the band needed to make a demo tape and had almost no idea how to go about it —but it was too late for that now. Instead she pulled the latest issue of *Rock Rag* out from under her arm and said, "The magazine looks great. Lots better than the last issue."

"Thanks. Since it's free, we have to get a lot of advertising to survive. Last month I spent hours running around to all the local stores and clubs, getting them to buy some space, and it really paid off. This month, I don't know. I have to do all the editing and most of the writing. I won't have time to look for advertising."

"What about him?" Robin asked, pointing to the boy in the red beret. He was sitting at one of the tables, hunched over some papers.

"Eddie has a night job in a restaurant on Bleecker Street. In his spare time he helps with paste-up and delivers some of the issues. He doesn't have time to look for advertising."

That was exactly what she'd been hoping to hear. "Actually, I could use a little extra money until this Backstage Records deal comes through. Maybe I could work for you, selling advertising or whatever."

Ian looked skeptical. "Do you have any experience?"

"Well, no," Robin said, deciding it was best to steer clear of any more lies, "but I'm sure I could do it. Besides, I could help in other ways too. I can type and I could answer the phone."

"We don't *have* a phone."

"Oh. Well, whatever." She looked up at Ian and shrugged. "Whaddaya think?"

He frowned. "Right now this magazine spends every penny it makes. Eddie and I are only taking home lunch money. All I could offer you is a small commission—ten percent of the advertising money you bring in."

Robin didn't hesitate. "I'll take it," she said eagerly.

Ian smiled broadly and Robin felt a wave of happiness rush over her. "Welcome to *Rock Rag*. What do you say we send Eddie out for some coffee to seal the deal? Meanwhile I can start showing you around."

Secretly Robin wished it could wait until another time, when she wasn't dressed like a middle-aged housewife and her hair wasn't drying into a frizzy mop. Still, she wasn't about to say no—not now, when

Ian was smiling at her like that. "Sure," she said, trying to sound relaxed and casual. "Sounds good."

While Ian walked over to talk to Eddie, Robin looked around the room, exulting in her incredible good luck. Without even trying she'd landed a job on a New York rock 'n' roll magazine. Okay, so it wasn't exactly *Rolling Stone,* but Robin wasn't complaining. After all, *Rock Rag* had something that *Rolling Stone* didn't. An editor named Ian Harkin.

|||||||||||||||||||||||||| **4**

C.C. was sitting cross-legged on her bed, staring idly at a *Happy Days* rerun and thinking about Kurt. She'd seen him twice since he told her he was going to Europe, and outwardly at least, their relationship hadn't changed. They still talked and laughed and drove into the city every chance they got. But under the surface, things were different, at least from her point of view. It's like that Pat Benatar song, she decided, the one that goes "I'm gonna harden my heart." That's what she was doing. Hardening her heart, so that no one— not even Kurt—could make it break.

Hearing the front door open C.C. turned down the TV. A peal of carefree laughter rang out through the house, followed by a crash, a muffled curse, and a giggle. C.C. nodded ruefully. She knew what those sounds meant. One, her mother was home, and two, she was drunk.

Tears would probably come later, but for the moment Mrs. Collins was in a good mood, and C.C. was ready to make the most of it. Hurriedly she pulled off her black jersey with the studs on the sleeves and slipped on a pale-blue monogrammed sweater. Fixing a smile on her face she stepped out of her room and walked down the hallway to the foyer.

Mrs. Collins was standing unsteadily in the doorway, her arms filled with the spoils of her latest shopping expedition. A large box from Bonwit Teller had fallen at her feet. Giggling softly, she stooped down to retrieve it.

"I'll get it, Mother," C.C. said, hurrying to help.

Startled, Mrs. Collins looked up, lost her balance, and fell back on her rear end with a resounding thud. Bags and boxes fell everywhere, spilling their contents onto the glossy hardwood floor. For an instant Mrs. Collins just sat there, wide eyed and open mouthed. Then, suddenly, she guffawed loudly and announced, "I fell flat on my derrière!"

C.C. forced herself to smile. "Let me help you," she said, hurrying over and offering a hand. "Are you all right?"

"Never been better," her mother replied, grunting as she staggered to her feet. "Just wait till you see what I bought for you."

Together they collected the fallen packages and carried them into the living room. "Open the Bloomie's bag," Mrs. Collins instructed, walking over to the sideboard and pouring herself some brandy from a half-empty bottle.

"You don't need another drink," C.C. said softly. "Just take off your coat and sit down."

"I intend to do just that," she answered breezily, stretching her arms out behind her so the coat slid off onto the floor. Picking up her brandy glass she walked across the room and collapsed onto the sofa next to C.C. "Go on, Catherine, open the bag."

C.C. tried to feign interest, but it wasn't easy. She hated the clothes her mother picked out for her—expensive but bland Evan-Picone dresses and tailored J. G. Hook pants, so different from the outrageous leather rock 'n' roll clothes she liked to wear. Opening the bag she pulled out a simple gray dress with a low back and long sleeves. "Uh, thanks," C.C. told her mother, "but I don't really need another dress."

"Oh, yes, you do," Mrs. Collins cooed, kicking off her heels and resting her feet on the mahogany coffee table. "Cynthia Biddle is having a housewarming party next Saturday evening. She and her husband just moved into the city. You can invite Kurt and—"

"Mother," C.C. said, trying to keep her voice light and cheerful, "I don't think I can make it. The band's starting to rehearse together again and I'm going to be awfully busy."

Her mother sat up and carelessly lowered her brandy glass onto the coffee table. Brandy sloshed over the side and dripped onto the Persian rug. Oblivious, she turned to C.C. "You'll never get anywhere with that attitude, young lady. Your coming out party was just a beginning. Now it's up to you to get out there and cultivate the contacts you've made." She patted her frosted blond hair and threw C.C. a conspiratorial glance. "Just remember, if your father marries that woman—"

"Bonnie?" C.C. asked, wondering what her father's new girlfriend was like. All she knew was that Bonnie was a widow and she lived in Connecticut. C.C. pictured a Jackie Onassis look-alike with oversized sunglasses and windblown hair, standing on the deck of her yacht.

"Yes, *her*. She's trying to get every penny of his

money for herself, Catherine. My lawyer says she can't do it, but I'm not so sure. We have to look out for ourselves. It's up to you to find someone who can take care of you, someone who'll give you the best."

C.C. thought about Kurt, then immediately pushed him out of her mind. Sighing, she looked at her mother. It was always like this when she drank too much. She started out giggly and carefree, but after a while something reminded her of Bonnie. That's when she started to freak out, whining and complaining and eventually yelling, until she burst into tears and staggered off to bed.

But C.C. couldn't afford to let that happen now. Not tonight, when she had something important to ask. "You're right, Mother," she said soothingly. "I will go to Mrs. Biddle's party. Actually, it sounds like fun." She stood up and held the dress up to her. "It's beautiful. Thank you!"

Mrs. Collins smiled and took a long swig of brandy. "I couldn't decide what dress to choose for myself, so I bought three. 'Charge it to Robert B. Collins,' I told them." She laughed loudly. "If he's going to walk out on *me,* he's going to have to pay."

C.C. tossed her new dress on the coffee table and sat down. "Mother," she began cautiously, "I have a favor to ask you."

"What is it, dear?"

"I—I need some money. You see, the band needs equipment, and we have to make a demo tape to send to record companies and . . . well, if I just had five hundred dollars . . ."

Mrs. Collins's eyes widened in alarm. "Five hundred dollars!" She frowned. "Catherine, you know I don't approve of this rock group you're in. I never did."

"But, Mother, the band is important to me. Singing with Overnight Sensation is all I want to do."

Mrs. Collins shook her head. "You'll never find a decent husband in that crowd."

C.C. knew that arguing would only make things worse, but she couldn't help herself. "I'm not looking for a husband. I'm still a teenager, for Chrissakes!"

Mrs. Collins's eyes were flashing. Jumping up she stood in front of C.C., swaying slightly. "Don't use that tone of voice with me, young lady. If you don't want to get married, go to college. Your father would gladly pay to send you to a good school."

"But I don't want to go to school," C.C. insisted. "I want to play rock 'n' roll!"

"Well, then, you'll get no money from me," her mother said grandly. Gulping down the last of the brandy she walked over to the sideboard and poured some more.

"Okay," C.C. said softly. "Then I'll just have to get a job."

Mrs. Collins spun around, still clutching the brandy bottle. "Don't you dare! I know your father's just waiting for an excuse to cut off his child-support payments. He wants to leave me without a penny, but I won't let him. I'm not going to give up this house and move into one of those lousy prefab apartment buildings. I won't do it!" The brandy bottle dropped from her hand and a puddle of dark liquid seeped onto the carpet.

C.C. didn't move. "Mother," she pleaded, "I really need the money."

"Don't you understand?" her mother shouted. "I don't *have* any money to give you!" Suddenly she hung her head and let out a choked sob. "I spent it."

"What?" C.C. asked incredulously. "What did you say?"

"I spent it. January's alimony check and February's too. We won't have another penny until your father sends the next check in March." She smiled moistly. "But don't worry. There's still the MasterCard and the Visa and—"

C.C. didn't wait to hear anymore. She ran out of the living room and into the foyer. Her camel's-hair coat was the first thing she saw when she opened the closet, so she threw it on and grabbed her purse. Biting her lower lip she forced herself to ignore the gulping sobs coming from the living room. Sorry, Mom, she thought sadly, you're going to have to take care of yourself tonight. Buttoning her coat she opened the front door and stepped out into the corridor. There was only one thing left to do. She had to go talk to her father.

It was almost eight-thirty by the time C.C. stepped off the train in Westport, Connecticut. She had spent most of the trip regretting her decision to come, and now, looking across the empty tracks at the station, she considered forgetting the whole thing and just catching the next train back to the city.

After all, she told herself, I have no idea if Daddy's going to be glad to see me. I don't even know if he's home.

Opening her purse she pulled out a crumpled piece of paper. It was the only communication she'd had from her father since her coming-out party—a short letter giving his new address and phone number in Westport and promising to invite her for a visit as soon as he'd "settled in."

She sighed. Why didn't I just wait until tomorrow and call Daddy at his office? she asked herself. It was dumb to come all the way out here. But part of her said, Why not? He's your father, isn't he? He can't turn you away.

C.C. walked over to the station. The three or four other people who had gotten off the train were getting into their cars and pulling away. Out front a lone taxi-cab waited across the street. She hurried over and got in.

Downtown Westport was a small confluence of styl-ish restaurants and shops with names like the Starfish Café and the Book Nook. Within minutes the taxi had left the streetlights behind and headed down a dark, tree-lined country road, dotted with large, stately houses. Another turn took them onto a narrow private road. Flipping on his brights the taxi driver continued until they came to a long, low house of stone and glass, nestled in among the trees.

"Here you go, miss."

C.C. paid the driver and stepped out into the dirt driveway. The front of the house was dark, but she could see lights in the back. Well, she told herself, it's too late to turn back now. Making her way to the front door she felt for the bell and pushed hard.

The door opened and C.C. found herself looking into the face of a red-haired woman in gray wool slacks and a stylish burnt-orange sweater.

"Oh, hi," C.C. stammered. "Uh, does Robert Col-lins live here?"

"Why, yes. May I tell him who's calling?"

"C.C. I mean, Catherine." The woman looked con-fused. "Catherine *Collins.*"

"Oh! You're Bob's daughter?" C.C. nodded shyly. "Oh, my! I'm Bonnie. Bonnie Dewhurst. Come right in. I'll tell Bob you're here."

C.C. stepped into the living room and glanced dis-tractedly at the low, Oriental-style furniture and the abstract paintings. I certainly didn't expect to find *her* here, she thought uncomfortably. In the other room she could make out the television and her father asking, "Who was it, sweetheart?"

Sweetheart. It had been a long time since she'd heard her father call her mother that. Actually he'd been away on business trips so much during the last few years, she couldn't remember him calling her anything at all.

"Cathy!"

C.C. looked up to see her father striding toward her. When he smiled, she forgot her worries and ran to meet him. "Daddy!" she cried, throwing herself into his arms.

He hugged her, then stepped back. "What are you doing here? Are you all right?"

C.C. nodded, blushing a little. "Yes. I'm sorry to bother you, but . . . well, I need to talk to you."

"Come into the den."

The den had pine paneling and floor-to-ceiling windows, but it was too dark outside to see anything except the vague outline of some trees. Mr. Collins flipped off the television and joined Bonnie on the leather couch. C.C. sat across from them on a matching leather chair.

"I've heard so much about you," Bonnie said in a cheery voice.

C.C. looked her over. She was a petite woman—a good ten years younger than Mr. Collins—with short red hair, delicate features, and creamy white skin. There was nothing wrong with her, really, but C.C. was determined to dislike her anyway. After all, it was because of Bonnie that her parents were divorced and her mother was drinking. "I didn't know you were shacking up with my dad," she said sullenly.

Mr. Collins glared at her. "Cathy, that's uncalled for!"

"I'm sorry," she said, feeling instantly guilty. No matter how much she hated Bonnie, she didn't want to hurt her father. She loved him too much.

"I'll get us something to drink," Bonnie suggested tactfully.

After she'd left, C.C. took a good look at her father. He was wearing navy slacks and a plaid madras shirt. Even though it was January, he had a dark tan. His hair had been graying at the temples, but now, she noticed, it was all dark brown.

He must be dyeing it, C.C. realized. Suddenly she felt sorry for her father. It must be tough trying to keep up with someone ten years younger, she thought, especially someone as good looking as Bonnie.

"Well, Cathy, what do you want to talk about?" Mr. Collins asked.

C.C. took a deep breath. This wasn't going to be easy. "Well, it's Mother. She's been drinking a lot, and tonight she told me she spent all the money you sent her for January and February."

Mr. Collins frowned and muttered an angry "Damn!" Then he sighed and shook his head. "Well, I guess I'm not surprised. Your mother's never been too stable. Still, you'd think with a daughter to take care of, she'd try to straighten up."

C.C. didn't know what to say. Unstable? She'd never thought of her mother that way. Now she wondered if it was true. "Do you think she's having a nervous breakdown or something?" C.C. asked with concern.

"Who knows?" he said with exasperation. "She's already tried everything else to get me back, why not that?" He paused and looked at her pained expression. "I'm sorry," he said quickly. "I didn't mean to be unkind. It's just that, well, this couldn't come at a worse time. Business is lousy, I've got debts coming out of my ears, and when the divorce trial comes up, your mother's going to take me to the cleaners. I just don't have time to worry about her personal problems. I've got enough of my own."

"But what about me?" C.C. blurted out. "I've got to live with her, and when she's loaded, I've got to take care of her, too. I think that really stinks!"

Mr. Collins cleared his throat. "Uh, Cathy," he said uncomfortably, "you know I'd love to have you here, but it just wouldn't work out. I'm in the city half the time and Bonnie only comes up on weekends. Besides, you wouldn't like it out here. It's too isolated, too . . ."

Mr. Collins was still talking, but C.C. wasn't listening. Is that what I wanted? she wondered. Was I hoping he'd ask me to come live with him out here? Maybe. Of course, she knew all the things her father was saying were true. She didn't want to live in Westport. Still, it would have felt good to hear him offer, instead of falling all over himself to make up excuses for not wanting her.

"You're right, Daddy," she said softly. "It wouldn't work out."

Mr. Collins looked relieved. "Oh," he said, looking up, "here's Bonnie with the drinks."

Bonnie handed C.C. a mug of hot chocolate and sat down. Everybody sipped in silence for a moment. Then Mr. Collins looked up. "Well, Cathy, considering the circumstances, I think the best thing for you would be to go off to college. Have you given any thought to where you—"

C.C. shook her head. "I don't want to go to college. Not now, anyway."

"Why not?" Bonnie asked, looking a little shocked.

"I'm the lead singer in a rock band," C.C. told her. "We're called Overnight Sensation. A guy at Back-street Records is interested in us, too, but he wants to hear a demo tape before he'll sign us." Carried away by her own enthusiasm she looked at her father and said, "That's why I need money. We have to buy equipment and rent studio time. If I just had a few hundred dollars . . ."

Bonnie's eyes narrowed. "Did your mother send you here?" she said suspiciously. "Did she tell you to ask your father for money?"

"What?" C.C. asked incredulously. "Of course not!"

Mr. Collins put his arm around Bonnie and gave her a reassuring pat. "Cathy," he said seriously, "I realize you need to get away from your mother, and I want to help. However, I'm really in no position to start investing in an amateur rock 'n' roll band. Now, if you want to go to college—"

"No way," C.C. said firmly.

"Then maybe it's time you found a job and moved out on your own. I'll be glad to give you something to get you started, but after that I think you should try to make it by yourself. After all, you're almost eighteen and it's about time you learned to work for what you want." He smiled paternally and added, "Of course, if you change your mind about going to school . . ."

C.C. didn't answer. What was there to say? For a long moment the room was silent. Then Bonnie cleared her throat and said, "It's too late to go home tonight, so I've made up the bed in the guest room for you. Shall I show you where it is?"

C.C. shrugged apathetically and stood up. Her father leaned forward and raised his head, as if expecting a kiss, but she was in no mood to oblige. Sorry, Daddy, she thought sadly. I'm not buying that loving-father routine anymore. Blinking the tears from her eyes she turned and followed Bonnie out of the room.

Later that night C.C. lay in bed, listening to the bare trees scrape against the windowpane. It reminded her of when she was a little girl and she used to be frightened by the dark silhouette of trees outside her bedroom window. Back then she only had to call out and her parents would come running to comfort her. Her mother would put her arms around her, and her father would tell her a silly bedtime story to make her laugh. But now C.C.'s mother was miles away in Short Hills, probably passed out on the living-room sofa. Her father was only in the next room, but as far as she was concerned, he might as well have been on another planet. If only Kurt . . . but no, she couldn't count on him anymore either.

From now on, she thought, I'm on my own. Pulling the covers over her head she curled up into a little ball and closed her eyes. It was dark and warm and quiet under there, and after a while she fell asleep.

 5

As the subway clattered out of the tunnel, Robin turned in her seat and looked out at the grimy warehouses and smelly factories that lined Brooklyn's Gowanus Canal. Although she'd grown up in New York City, Robin had rarely been to Brooklyn. There had never been any reason to go there—that is, until the band started practicing at Annette's high school.

Now she took the subway through the Brooklyn Battery Tunnel two or three times a week. She still didn't know Brooklyn very well, but she was intimately acquainted with every stop on the F train between Greenwich Village and Carroll Street.

Today, the girls were meeting at a Union Street coffee shop for lunch before heading over to Annette's school for their Saturday afternoon practice session. Robin got off the subway and headed down Carroll Street, vainly trying to ignore the painful blister on her right foot.

Maybe I shouldn't have taken the job at *Rock Rag,* she thought for at least the hundredth time that week. Somehow I'd imagined that working for a music magazine would be exciting. I mean, it's not as if I expected Mick Jagger to drop by the office and ask me out to lunch or anything, but, gee, I had no idea it was going to be such hard work.

Robin sighed. It was hard to believe, but after a week of walking into practically every shop, restaurant, and office in the East Village, she'd only sold two lousy ads. The magazine made one hundred dollars, and that meant a ten-dollar commission for her. Ten dollars and a couple of blisters for an entire week of pounding the pavement. What a drag!

Still, there was one thing that made the job worthwhile: Ian. Whenever Robin sold an ad or just got tired of striking out, she hurried back to the office to see him. Mostly they just drank coffee and talked about the magazine or the latest news on the rock scene. Not exactly deep personal stuff. But every now and then she noticed Ian looking at her in a way that suggested he saw her as more than just another *Rock Rag* employee. When that happened, Robin's stomach did a flip-flop, her heart raced, and she usually did something totally dumb like giggle or spill her coffee.

That was the extent of their relationship so far, but, well, it was a start.

Robin walked on, thinking about Ian, until she saw the neon sign for the Roma Coffee Shop. Inside, C.C. was waving at her from an empty booth. Waving back, Robin walked over to join her. "Hi," she said. "Where's Gail and Annette?"

"They're not here yet."

"Oh," Robin muttered, feeling a little awkward. It was silly to feel uncomfortable around C.C., she knew, but she couldn't help it. The two of them had never gotten along all that well. Right from the beginning they'd disagreed about practically everything, especially when it came to Reg and his management of the band. What made it even worse was that while Robin was putting Reg down, C.C. was falling in love with him. Of course, all that was history now. C.C. had dumped Reg and returned to Overnight Sensation. Even so, Robin couldn't help feeling that C.C. held her responsible for messing up their big chance at stardom.

Robin grabbed a menu from behind the napkin dispenser and pretended she was deciding what to order. With any luck Annette and Gail would show up soon and they could all fall into their usual light banter and easy laughter.

"Robin?"

Robin glanced up from the menu. As always C.C. looked terrific. Her long blond hair had been pulled to one side and braided with strands of red and blue ribbons. Blue triangular earrings bounced lightly against her cheeks and highlighted her clear blue eyes. Her black jersey and red tank top fit snugly around her torso, and her Guess? jeans looked as if they'd been painted on.

Robin looked down at her own outfit and sighed.

This morning faded gray cords and a denim shirt had seemed like a great choice. Now, next to C.C., she felt like a total slob. "What is it?" she asked, unable to keep the irritation out of her voice.

C.C. didn't seem to notice. "You know that idea you had about us all moving in together?"

"Yeah?"

"Well, I think it sounds great. In fact, I think we should do it right now."

Robin pushed the menu aside and shook her head. "We can't. Not now, anyway. Gail and Annette won't be out of high school until June. Besides," Robin added, "I thought you didn't like the idea. You said we'd all be at each other's throats."

C.C. shrugged. "I changed my mind." Looking Robin in the eye she said eagerly, "Maybe Annette and Gail have to wait until June, but we don't. We could start looking for a place right now."

Robin laughed nervously. The intensity in C.C.'s voice surprised her. "But I don't have any money," she said.

C.C. reached into her purse and pulled out a check. Laying it in front of Robin she said simply, "I do."

The check was made out to Catherine Christine Collins, and when Robin read the amount, her mouth fell open. "Two thousand dollars!" she gasped. "C.C., where did you get this?"

C.C. looked a little embarrassed. "From my father. It's sort of a birthday present. I'll be eighteen next week, you know."

Robin let out a long, low whistle. "Wow! When I turned eighteen, all I got was a Walkman and a couple of tapes!"

C.C. put her elbows on the table and leaned forward. "Robin, listen! We can use this money to get an apartment. By the time it's all spent, we'll both have jobs and we can split the rent. Then when Annette and Gail graduate, they can move in too. It'll be perfect. Come on, Robin. Say yes."

Robin didn't answer. Of course she wanted to get an apartment. She'd been thinking about it ever since the band got back together. But in her imagination it had been all four of them living there, not just C.C. and her. "What about the band?" Robin asked, stalling for time. "We have to use our money for equipment and recording, not on an apartment."

"But if the apartment also doubles as a practice space, then it helps the band too."

Robin looked away. What am I so worried about? she asked herself. Now that Reg is out of the picture, there's no reason for me and C.C. not to get along.

But Robin knew that wasn't what was really bothering her. The truth was, she was jealous of C.C. She always had been, ever since that first day Reg brought the girls together. I know it's stupid, Robin told herself, but I can't help it. C.C. seems to have everything. She's beautiful, she's got loads of money, and she can get any guy she wants. When the band's up onstage, she's the center of attention. I write the songs, I play lead guitar, but nobody even notices me. They're too busy looking at her.

If we had an apartment together, she fretted, it would be even worse. C.C.'d always be bringing home new clothes and making herself gorgeous, while I'd be too broke to buy a new pair of sneakers. And there'd be boys around all the time, swooning over her and ignoring me.

"I don't think you and me living together is such a good idea," Robin muttered, shaking her head.

"Why not?" C.C. asked.

Robin looked down at her hands. "I don't know,"

she lied. "Maybe I'm just not as eager to move out on my own as I thought I was."

C.C. didn't answer. When the silence got unbearable, Robin looked up. C.C. had her elbows on the table and her head in her hands. Is she mad? Robin wondered. She looked closer. C.C.'s lips were trembling. "C.C.," Robin asked, reaching out to touch her arm, "what's wrong?"

C.C. shook her head. "It's nothing," she said in a small, unsteady voice. "Forget it."

A waitress approached the booth, but Robin motioned her away. Leaning across the table she said softly, "C.C., please tell me. I'm sorry if I said something wrong. Really I am."

C.C. looked up. "It's not your fault," she said. "It's just, well, it's just that things aren't too great around my house these days. My mother's been blowing her alimony payments on shopping sprees and booze, and my father doesn't want me to live with him. He gave me that check so I could move out on my own, but . . . oh, Robin, I'm scared! I never lived away from my parents before." She picked up a fork from the table and fingered it nervously. "That's why I thought it would be so terrific if you and I could find an apartment. I mean, you're always so together, Robin. You know what you want and how to get it. Not like me. I'm so confused and insecure and . . ." She wiped a tear off her cheek with the back of her hand and let out an exasperated sigh. "Oh, God, now I'm crying in the middle of the Roma Coffee Shop. I could just die!"

Robin stared at C.C., dumbstruck. "C.C.," she managed to say, "are you serious? Ever since we met, I've been jealous of you because you're so beautiful and hip and uninhibited. The only reason I said I didn't want to live with you is because I thought it would drive me crazy, constantly comparing myself to you and coming up second best."

C.C. laughed through her tears. "Robin, you must be nuts! You're the one people are jealous of. You can play the guitar and write incredible songs, and you know more about rock 'n' roll than Annette and Gail and me put together."

"Gee." Robin smiled sheepishly. "Thanks."

The waitress appeared again. "This isn't Prospect Park, girls. You can't sit here unless you order something."

"We're waiting for our friends," Robin told her. She turned to C.C. "What happened to Annette and Gail?"

"I told them to come a half hour late because I needed to talk to you." She turned to the waitress. "Coffee, please."

Robin nodded. "Me too."

The waitress rolled her eyes. "Teenagers!" she muttered as she walked away.

Robin giggled and looked at C.C. When their eyes met, she said, "C.C., do you really think we could live together?"

"I don't know," C.C. answered earnestly, stuffing the check back into her purse. "But I'd like to give it a try."

Robin nodded thoughtfully. "Okay," she said with a shrug. "Why not?"

C.C. let out a squeal of joy. "Oh, Robin," she cried, "this is going to be great. I just know it!" She reached into her purse and pulled out a folded newspaper. "Now, I have the real estate section right here. There's a place in Chelsea that sounds like a possibility and—"

Robin laughed. "Hold on. I've got to talk to my parents first. They know I want to move out, but they figured it would be in June, not right this minute."

Before C.C. could answer, the waitress brought their coffee. "I think your friends are here," she said, motioning toward the door. Robin turned around. Gail and Annette were making their way across the crowded restaurant, waving enthusiastically.

"Hi, there!" Annette called. She slid in beside C.C., and Gail sat next to Robin. "Good news. I think I got a job. It's at a branch of the Brooklyn Public Library, filing catalog cards and shelving books. There was a notice up at my school, so I ran right over. They made me alphabetize about five hundred catalogue cards to see if I could do it right. It was boring but pretty easy. I'll find out on Monday if I got the job."

"Great!" Robin exclaimed. "I got a job, too, but I don't know if it's going to work out. I'm selling ads for a rock 'n' roll magazine called *Rock Rag*.

"*Rock Rag?*" Annette repeated. "Isn't that where Ian Harkin works?"

"Uh, yeah," Robin admitted. "He's the editor."

"Ah-ha!" Annette exclaimed. "I had a feeling you were interested in him. No wonder you wanted to work there."

"Ooh," Gail squealed, "he's cute!"

Robin could feel herself blushing. "Yeah, he is, isn't he?"

The waitress hovered near the booth and everyone ordered. "My news isn't so good," Gail said when they were alone again. "I asked my brother about that friend of his who plays the piano at a ballet school. It seems she just lucked into the job because her aunt teaches at the school. Anyway, I went through the phone book and called up every ballet school I could find. No luck. Either they already have someone, or they use tapes."

"Well, don't give up," Robin told her. "Maybe you

can find some other way to make money by playing the piano."

"You could give piano lessons," C.C. suggested.

"Or play in restaurant," Annette said. "You know, one of those fancy places where they have live music in the background. Or a bar where they have sing-alongs."

Gail looked worried. "I don't think my parents would be very happy about that."

"What about you, C.C.?" Annette asked. "Did you find a job?"

C.C. lit a cigarette. "Better than that," she said with a grin. "My father gave me an early birthday present." She looked at Robin as if to say, *The real story is a secret between me and you.* Pulling the check out of her purse she showed it to Annette and Gail. Ignoring their amazed stares she announced, "Robin and I are going to use the money to get an apartment together."

"You and Robin?" Annette said incredulously. "Are you serious?"

Robin laughed. In the past she had often complained to Annette about C.C. No doubt C.C. had also complained to Annette about Robin. It was no wonder Annette found the idea of them living together a little unbelievable. "We're serious," Robin assured her. "We're going to try to find an apartment that can double as a practice space. And in June you and Gail can both move in."

"Listen," C.C. broke in. "I just had a flash. We aren't going to need this entire two thousand dollars to rent an apartment, are we?"

Robin shrugged. "Who knows? I never looked for an apartment before."

"Well, I think we should spend some of it on the band." She paused dramatically. "What does Overnight Sensation need more than anything else?"

All three girls answered at once. "A bass guitar!"

"Right. So what are we waiting for? Let's go buy one."

Gail stared wide eyed at C.C. "Could we really?"

C.C. nodded. "Why not? We'll go cash this check and start looking."

Just then the waitress arrived with the food. "Where's the check?" Annette asked, ignoring the hamburger that had just been set in front of her. "We're in a hurry!"

The waitress shook her head. "Mother of God! First you sit around like you got all the time in the world. Now you act like your pants are on fire." She dropped the check on the table and walked off muttering, "Teenagers!"

The girls dissolved into giggles. C.C. choked on her coffee and the others had to pound her on the back. "Let's ask the waitress if she'd mind coming over here and doing a Heimlich maneuver on you," Robin suggested, and C.C. laughed even harder.

They started to leave, but C.C. had left her two-thousand-dollar check on the table and had to run back to get it. "I've heard of big tips," Annette said dryly, "but that's ridiculous!"

By now C.C. was giddy with laughter. Ignoring the stares of the other diners Robin dragged her away from the booth and led her toward the door. "Make way!" Robin cried. "This is an emergency. We've got a case of third-degree giggles here. If we don't get this girl someplace serious, there's no telling what might happen!"

When she'd finally caught her breath, C.C. looked at Robin and said, "You know, I think we're going to have a good time living together."

Robin paused, thinking it over. Despite all the nice things she and C.C. had just said to each other, there was no telling how well they'd be able to get along on a day-to-day basis. What if C.C. was a real slob, or even worse, a neatness freak? What if she wanted to have wild parties all the time or what if she couldn't find a job and wasn't able to pay the rent? Robin didn't know the answer to those or any of the other ten thousand questions that filled her head. There was just no way she could predict the future. All she knew was that right now, looking for an apartment with C.C. felt right.

Robin put her arm around C.C. and gave her an affectionate squeeze. "Come on, roommate," she said with a smile. "Let's go cash that check."

 6

Gail plugged her new bass guitar into the tiny practice amp and plucked a few experimental notes. Not bad! Of course, it was just a beat-up secondhand Yamaha, a real clunker compared to the Fender Precision Bass Reg had once given her to play. Still, it was better than nothing, and nothing is exactly what she'd had until C.C. laid out the money for this one.

Gail stopped playing and cocked her head, listening intently. Except for the hum of the refrigerator the house was silent. Lying back across her bed she made a mental checklist of her family's whereabouts. Her parents were still at work—her father at his computer-programing job for Hammond, Inc., and her mother at a new part-time cashier job at the local 7-Eleven. Jessie had orchestra rehearsal at Juilliard, and her younger brother, Garrett, was at his weekly violin lesson across town. None of them would be home for at least an hour.

With a relieved sigh she cranked up the volume on her amplifier. When she started to play, the thumping bass lines filled the bedroom and shook the windows. Closing her eyes she put her fingers on automatic pilot and let her mind run free.

Six months ago, she realized, she would never have believed that being home alone could make her so happy. Back then she liked nothing better than to be around her family, especially when they were making music. In those days her dream was to go to the Juilliard School of Music and become a classical pianist. Nothing, she knew, would please her parents more.

But then she joined Overnight Sensation. Her parents were furious, and for a while Gail tried to forget about the band and return to her classical studies. But it was no use. She'd fallen in love with rock 'n' roll. Finally, with the help of her piano teacher, Mr. Dawson, she convinced her parents to let her stay in the group. She was still planning to go to Juilliard in September, but only as a part-time student.

Gail sighed. She loved her family and she knew they loved her too. Nonetheless she could feel herself drifting farther and farther away from them. *I can't live up to their expectations,* she thought sadly. *If only they could learn to accept me as I am.* . . .

An odd buzzing sound interrupted Gail's thoughts. Glancing down she saw the problem. The G string on her bass was coming unwound. It wasn't all that surprising, really. The strings had been on the instrument when she bought it, and they were probably months— maybe even years—old.

Gail glanced at her bedside clock. Four-fifteen. Jessie and Garrett would be home soon. It seemed like a good time to go to the music store and buy some new strings. Putting down her bass she ran a wire comb through her short Afro until it looked full and even. Her simple forest-green turtleneck seemed too plain by itself, so she added a gray wool sweater-vest with a row of pink hearts across the chest.

Grabbing her coat and backpack Gail left the house and walked the four blocks to the nearest bus stop. When the bus appeared, she paid her fare and took a seat near the back. The bus was empty except for a few elderly ladies with shopping bags, and half a dozen white teenage girls. She didn't recognize the girls, but they were talking about the unbeaten record of the Columbia High basketball team, so she knew they must be from her school.

Gail leaned against the window and looked out at the traffic. In September, back when she'd first moved to New Jersey, she'd made a half hearted effort to join in. But these days she figured, why bother? This was her only year in the South Orange–Maplewood school system. Why should she try to overcome the triple stigmas of being shy, black, and a classical musician, just so she could make a few temporary friends? Besides, she didn't have time for basketball games or school dances. She had to devote herself to Overnight Sensation. That was where she belonged.

Ignoring the gossiping girls Gail stood up and walked to the front of the bus. When the driver turned onto Main Street, she got off and went into Burton's House of Music. After a few minutes greedily eyeing the expensive Steinberger basses hanging on the wall, she bought two sets of strings and turned to leave. That was when she noticed a bulletin board near the door. Pausing, she glanced at a few of the notices.

Most of them were messages from people selling instruments or offering their services to bands in need of new members. Nothing particularly interesting.

She was halfway out the door when a notice at the bottom of the bulletin board caught her eye. It was handwritten on a paper cocktail napkin. WANTED, it read. PIANO PLAYER FOR BERNARD'S. MUST KNOW A VARIETY OF STANDARDS AND CURRENT POP TUNES TO APPEAL TO OUR EVENING CROWD. CALL MAX. 555-1289.

Gail read the message again. She had no idea where or what Bernard's was, and she had to admit her repertoire of standards and current pop tunes was almost nil. Still, it was a job, and a musical one at that. It might even be fun.

Memorizing the number she walked to the pay phone across the street and dialed. It wasn't until the phone started ringing that she began to feel nervous. She was just about to hang up when a gruff male voice said, "Bernard's."

"Um, yes, h-hello," Gail stammered. "May I speak to Max?"

"That's me. What can I do for ya?"

"Oh. Well, I saw your ad for a piano player and, uh, well, I was wondering if you were still looking for someone."

"Yeah, sure. Listen, can ya come over right now and audition? We need someone to start this Friday night."

"Um, sure. I guess so. I mean, yes. But I don't know how to get there."

Max rattled off the directions. Bernard's was on the outskirts of Newark, just over the East Orange line. "See ya in a few minutes," Max said. Before she could answer, he'd hung up.

Gail pulled out another quarter and dialed home. Luckily Garrett answered the phone and she was able to leave, without a lengthy cross-examination, the message that she wouldn't be home for dinner. As soon as she'd hung up, she rushed back to the music store and searched through the songbooks for a compilation of pop tunes. *Favorite Songs from the Seventies* looked good, so she bought it and ran out to catch the bus that was pulling up across the street.

Forty-five minutes and two buses later she stood in front of Bernard's, trying to get up the nerve to go inside. The restaurant was on a busy highway crowded with fast-food joints, car washes, and auto-parts stores. It was an undistinguished concrete box, set back from the road and surrounded by a parking lot. A large neon sign near the road proclaimed this to be BERNARD'S SURF AND TURF. Beneath that were the words ENTERTAINMENT FRIDAY AND SATURDAY NIGHTS IN THE FISHNET LOUNGE.

Gail tried to imagine what her parents would say if they could see her now. It wasn't a very pleasant thought, so she hurried on to her next concern. If the people she had seen in the bus and on the streets were any indication, this was a white working-class neighborhood. How would the owners of Bernard's feel about hiring a seventeen-year-old black girl to play the piano in their restaurant?

Gail shivered as a frigid wind whipped around the building and blasted her full in the face. It was too cold to keep standing in the parking lot, and another bus wouldn't be by for at least half an hour. Well, I've come this far, she told herself. I might as well go in. If the place looks too creepy I can always leave.

Hesitantly she opened the heavy wooden door and walked inside. The restaurant was one large, dimly lit room with dark-red carpeting, wood paneling, and tables covered with white tablecloths. The walls were decorated with undistinguished paintings of seascapes and sunsets. Ten or fifteen people—all middle-aged and white—were sitting at the tables, eating and talking.

Gail was wondering what to do next, when a woman with heavy makeup and a bouffant hairdo walked up. "One?" she asked skeptically, clutching a pile of menus to her chest.

"Um, no, thank you," Gail muttered. "I mean, I'm not here for dinner. I'm supposed to talk to Max."

"Oh. Right through there," the woman said, pointing to a large entranceway off to the left. Gail hadn't noticed it before, but now she could see it led to the lounge. An oval-shaped bar draped with fishnets was visible, as well as a few small tables.

"Thank you," Gail said, walking slowly into the lounge. She knew it was silly, but bars scared her. They were dark and mysterious places, dens of evil and corruption, if her father was to be believed.

"Can I help ya, hon?" The bartender was leaning against the bar, looking her over. He was a burly man, around forty, with thinning hair and a dark beard.

"I'm looking for Max," she said.

He smiled with one side of his mouth. "That's me."

"Oh, hi. I just talked to you on the phone. I play the piano."

Max's eyes widened. "That was you, huh?" He looked Gail up and down. "How old are ya, sweetheart?"

"Seventeen."

"Just a kid." He pointed to an old paint-chipped piano in the corner. "Well, show me what ya can do."

Flexing her fingers Gail sat down at the piano and hit a few experimental chords. Ugh! It was out of tune. All right, never mind, she told herself. This isn't Carnegie Hall. She opened *Favorite Songs of the Seventies* and started playing the first song in the book, "Take Me Home, Country Roads," by John Denver.

When the song was over, she looked at Max. He was waiting on a customer, so she turned the page and played the next song, Stevie Wonder's "You Are the Sunshine of My Life." When that ended, she looked up again. "Keep playing," Max said with an impatient wave of his hand.

Five songs later he walked over and leaned against the piano. "Okay, I guess you'll do. Friday and Saturday nights, eight to midnight. Thirty dollars a night. You'll have to go to the police station and get fingerprinted. Make sure ya do that this week."

"Fingerprinted?" Gail asked nervously. "Why?"

"For the permit. You're underage, so ya gotta get a permit to work here. What's yer name, hon?"

"Gail. Gail Harrison."

"Okay. And make sure ya don't play none of that soul music. The customers don't go for that kinda stuff, okay?"

"Uh, sure. Okay."

"Right. Also, this songbook's gotta go. Memorize twenty or thirty songs and you can fake the rest. Got it?"

Gail nodded distractedly. She was thinking about all the money she was going to be making. Just wait till I tell the girls, she thought happily. Sixty dollars a week! If I keep this up, we'll be in the studio in no time.

"I'll see ya Friday night," Max was saying. "Be here by seven forty-five and bring the permit." He paused. "Oh, and come in the back entrance, by the kitchen. You can leave that way too." He turned and walked back to the bar. "So long, hon."

Gail put away her music and walked to the back of the restaurant. A set of swinging double doors led to the kitchen. As she stepped forward to push them in, both doors flew outward. With a gasp Gail leaped backward and just missed being hit in the face.

"Hey! You all right?" She looked up and found herself gazing into the dark-brown eyes of a very attractive young man. He was tall and muscular, with full lips, a wide nose, and Michael Jackson curls. Even in his white bus-boy uniform he looked cool and cocky.

"Y-yes," Gail stammered, stepping back and straightening her coat. "I'm sorry."

"Me, too, but what you doin' back here, babe?"

The boy's slangy street talk made Gail a little wary. Back when she lived in The Bronx, her parents were always telling her to stay away from kids who talked like that. "I won't have my children picking up that street talk," her father used to say. "You'll never get anywhere in this world if you sound ignorant."

"Uh, I was just leaving," Gail said, stepping around him.

"Hey, chill out," he said, grabbing her arm. "You workin' here or somethin'?"

Gail turned to face him, intensely aware that his hand was still on her arm. She could feel her heart pounding, but she wasn't sure if it was from excitement or fear. "I will be. I'm going to be playing the piano in the lounge on Friday and Saturday nights."

The boy smiled, revealing a mouth full of dazzling white teeth. Releasing her arm he said, "They call me Flip-Flop 'cause I break-dance so good. Flip for short."

"I'm Gail," she answered shyly. Her arm still tingled where he'd touched it.

Flip held out his hand and Gail tried to shake it. But as soon as her hand was in his, he lifted it to his lips and kissed her knuckles. Gail felt her knees go weak. "I'm pleased to meet you, Miss Gail," he said softly, gazing up into her eyes.

Before she could answer, a waitress barged through the doors carrying a tray loaded with plates of food. "Get moving, Morris," she ordered brusquely. "Table four isn't going to clean itself."

"That's Flip," he yelled, releasing Gail's hand. *"Flip!"* He started after the waitress, then stopped and turned back to Gail. "I'll see you Friday, you pretty young thing."

"F-Friday," she repeated, her heart pounding in her ears. She watched as Flip walked away, hips swaying with each long, easy stride. When he was out of sight, she turned and walked unsteadily through the busy kitchen and out into the twilight.

The back of Bernard's was even uglier than the front, but to Gail the cracked blacktop and smelly dumpsters seemed wondrously beautiful. "Flip," she whispered breathlessly. "Friday night." Filled with a wild exhilaration she took off across the parking lot, laughing as the cold wind hit her face.

||||||||||||||||||||||| **7**

Robin opened the door of the Back to the Garden natural-foods store and walked inside. Jenny, one of her mother's employees, was at the front counter. "Where's Mom?" Robin asked, selecting a carob-and-coconut candy bar from the shelf and ripping open the wrapper.

"Knee deep in fruits and vegetables," Jenny answered. "Go on back."

Robin walked down the center aisle toward the back of the store, glancing at the packages of whole-grain pasta and all-natural fruit juices that lined the shelves. When she came upon some cans of seaweed stew, she grimaced and turned away. Some of this natural food stuff was too gross to believe!

Robin turned the corner and found her mother standing in the produce department, surrounded by boxes of fruits and vegetables. Her curly brown hair, just like Robin's only shorter, looked a little disheveled, and one side of her faded blue overalls had fallen off her shoulder.

"Hi, Mom," Robin greeted her.

Mrs. Quinn looked up. "Oh, Robin, am I glad to see you! Come help me with this stuff. My stock girl called in sick and I have to get everything on the shelves before it gets busy in here." She paused and pulled up the strap on her overalls. "Wait a minute."

"What?" Robin asked, swallowing her last mouthful of the carob-and-coconut candy bar.

"Aren't you supposed to be at school now? I thought you had classes on Friday mornings."

She shrugged. "Yeah, well, I do, but nothing really important. Just English 102 and Anthropology. English is a real gut and Anthro—"

"Robin," Mrs. Quinn said firmly, "I thought we agreed you were going to work harder this semester."

Robin nodded glumly. She'd finished her first semester at NYU with three C's and a D. Kind of embarrassing, especially since her father taught there. "I'm trying, Mom, but, jeez, I'm so busy. If I don't sell some more ads for *Rock Rag,* we'll never have enough money to make a demo."

"Listen, honey, I'm not asking you to give up your dream of being a rock musician. We just want you to be prepared in case things don't work out. That's what a college degree is all about."

"But, Mom, I can go to college anytime. Music won't wait. I mean, I can just see me calling up Backstage Records in four years and saying, 'Hi, remember me? I just finished college and now I'm ready to make a record.' " She laughed ruefully. "They already think Overnight Sensation is yesterday's news. We'd be last century's news by then."

Mrs. Quinn sighed. "All right. No more motherly advice today. But as long as you've already started this semester, just promise me you'll try to pull some decent grades. Okay?"

Robin nodded. "Okay."

"Good. Now help me with this produce. Just open that box of lettuce and pile it up in this bin. If any of the heads look rotten, leave them in the box." Relieved that the lecture was over, Robin set to work. "How's your job going?" her mother asked, stacking boxes of cherry tomatoes. "Make any sales this week?"

"A couple. Ian says it'll be a lot easier once the magazine gets a following. Right now, though, when I tell people I'm from *Rock Rag* they think I'm selling clothes."

"Why didn't you ask *me* for a job? You knew I was hiring some new people."

"Well . . ."

"Oh, I know," she said teasingly. "You'd rather work for some good-looking young magazine editor than for your dear, sweet old mom. I can't understand it, but teenagers are funny that way."

"Mom!" Robin could feel her cheeks turning red. "Come on!"

Mrs. Quinn laughed. "Sorry." She finished with the tomatoes and turned to Robin. "To what do I owe the pleasure of this visit? Not that I'm complaining, mind you. But if you have enough spare time to help me unpack produce, I should think you'd be able to find the time to check in on English 102 once in a while."

Robin smiled guiltily. "Well, actually, I wanted to ask you something. Mom"—she paused and took a deep breath—"How would you like to put an ad for the store in *Rock Rag?* They're cheap— only fifty dollars for a quarter of a page and a hundred for a half page. And it's for a good cause." She smiled sweetly and pointed at her chest. "Me."

Mrs. Quinn sighed. "Well, I guess I can't resist a pitch like that. Although I doubt the people who read *Rock Rag* are the natural-foods type. They're probably hardened punk rockers who survive on nothing but whiskey and beer nuts."

"Oh, Mom, come on! Gimme a break!"

"All right," she said with a smile. "Come on up front and I'll write you a check. I'll even let you design the ad. But just remember what I said about school. You had a B-plus average in high school. There's no reason why you can't do that at NYU."

Robin nodded, but her mind was on the check her mother was going to give her. Happily, she tossed a head of lettuce over her shoulder. It landed in one of the bins with a pleasing thunk. "Way to go, Quinn," she congratulated herself. Turning she followed her mother to the front of the store.

Clutching the check in her hand Robin hurried across town to the *Rock Rag* office to tell Ian she'd sold another ad. He had given her a key to the building, so she no longer had to knock and hope someone was around to hear her. Letting herself in she walked through the foyer and into the office.

No one was there. "Ian?" she called, just in case he was in the tiny bathroom in back. "Eddie?" No answer.

Frowning with disappointment Robin walked aimlessly across the room and sat down at the typewriter. This is where Ian sits, she told herself. It was silly, she knew, but sitting in the same chair that he had once occupied seemed sort of exciting. It was as if she could pick up the feel of his skin from the green plastic seat. Closing her eyes, she tried to imagine what it would be like to touch him. The thought of it made her feel hot and tingly all over.

Sighing, Robin glanced at the typewriter. There was a piece of paper in it, covered with text. She leaned over and read the first few lines. It was a review Ian was writing about the recently televised MTV rock video awards. Ian wrote well and Robin quickly found herself reading the whole thing. The text ended midsentence with the line "Despite strong competition from Pat Benatar and Tina Turner, the award for Best Video by a Female Artist was captured by—"

I know, thought Robin. Without thinking she straightened her chair and typed in "Cyndi Lauper. The video, costarring her mother and her boyfriend, effectively used Lauper's Betty Boop persona to illustrate the live-for-today message of the lyrics."

Hey, Robin thought proudly, that's pretty good. She paused a minute to think up what to write next, then started typing. She was just finishing up the last sentence when the door opened.

"Well, hello there." Robin spun around to see Ian standing in the doorway with his hands on his hips and a quizzical expression on his face. "What are you doing at my desk?" he asked.

Blushing with embarrassment Robin jumped up and blurted out the first thing she could think of. "Cyndi Lauper," she said.

Ian frowned. "What?"

"Uh, Cyndi Lauper. That's who won the award for Best Video by a Female Artist. I just thought I'd type it in for you."

"Oh." He walked over and pulled the page out of the typewriter. "I see you were generous enough to finish the rest of the article for me too."

"Well, uh . . . yeah." I had no right to be fooling around with Ian's article she thought miserably. Besides, he probably thinks the part I wrote is terrible. She glanced up as he was reading the end of the article and thought, He's probably right too. "I'm sorry," she muttered. "I was just fooling around."

She reached out to take the paper from Ian's hand, but he pulled it away. "It's good," he said with a small smile. "I didn't know you could write."

Robin was too relieved to be irritated by Ian's lack of confidence in her writing ability. "Thanks," she said modestly.

Ian paused thoughtfully, then asked, "Think you might be interested in writing some reviews for *Rock Rag?*"

Robin didn't even try to sound cool. "Are you kidding?" she cried. "I'd love it!"

"Okay, great. You can start your first assignment tonight. There's a band called Naming of Parts playing at the Townhouse. I want you to go check out their act and write a review."

"Naming of Parts?" Robin asked dubiously. "I never heard of 'em."

Ian smiled. "It's *my* band. Can you come?"

"Your band?" Robin repeated with amazement. "I didn't know you were in a band."

"I'm a man of many talents." Ian chuckled. "Magazine editor, record producer, rock star. Unfortunately none of my many glamorous jobs pays enough to support me. I'm barely making the rent each month." He shrugged. "The band is really my first love. Even if I couldn't make a cent, I'd still be doing that." He met her eye. "I'd really like you to hear us."

Robin felt her knees turn to Jell-O. "I'll be there," she said breathlessly.

Ian nodded and turned to sit on the desk. Swinging his long legs he asked, "In the meantime, how's sales?"

"Oh, that's what I came to tell you. I sold one to my mother this morning. She owns a natural-food store on Sixth Avenue." Robin pulled the check from her pocket and proudly handed it to Ian.

"Terrific!" He put the check behind him on the desk. "Are you going to try to sell any more ads this afternoon?"

"I can't. C.C. and I are trying to find an apartment we can move into together. She's coming by here in a little while to meet me. We're going to hit some of the real estate offices in the Village."

"Don't do that," Ian told her. "Those real estate guys'll rip you off. It's better to deal directly with the landlord. What kind of a place are you looking for?"

"Someplace we can practice in—and it's got to be cheap. Other than that, we're open to suggestions."

"Hmm. I don't know if you'd be interested, but there's a place upstairs that's open. Actually, since the top three floors are boarded up, it's the only other apartment in the building. The landlord just bought the place and I guess he's fixing it up floor by floor.

Anyway, some guy was going to move in up there, but he changed his mind. Wanna go look at it?"

"Yes!" she practically shouted. "Do you have a key?"

"It's not locked. There's nothing up there to steal. Come on."

Eagerly Robin followed Ian out of the office and up the narrow staircase to the second floor. The landing was littered with fallen plaster and broken glass. Stepping over it Ian walked to the door and pushed it open. "Uh, looks like it needs a little work," he announced, walking inside.

Robin followed. "Wow!" She gasped. "You're not kidding!" The place looked as if a bomb had recently been detonated in the middle of the floor. Dirty yellow wallpaper was peeling off the walls in long strips. Plaster had crumbled from the ceiling and spread white dust everywhere. The floor was made of rotting wood, painted brown and speckled with three or four other colors. On the plus side the room was large, the ceilings were high, and there were two large windows that faced out onto the street. Unfortunately two panes were missing. Still, the room was sunny and bright.

"Is there more?" she asked uncertainly.

"I think so." They turned left and walked to the end of the living room. A doorway led to a narrow hall. Off that was a small kitchen with ripped linoleum and a tiny, grease-covered stove. No refrigerator. Farther down the hallway was an even smaller, windowless bedroom that looked like a miniature version of the living room. Last stop was the bathroom. The water in the toilet was brown, and the old-fashioned sink and tub were covered with grit.

"Pretty gross," Robin said, wrinkling her nose.

"True. Still, it's got some important advantages. It's near the Village and the band could practice in it."

Yeah, thought Robin, and even more important, it's right upstairs from the *Rock Rag* office. If I lived here, I'd get to see Ian all the time. The thought was so exciting that Robin barely heard what Ian was saying. Something about the rent, she thought. She looked up at him. He was tall, probably six one or six two. Since Robin was five feet nine, and taller than most of the boys she'd ever dated, that was a real plus.

"What's the matter?" Ian asked. "Don't tell me you don't think that's a good price!"

"I'm sorry," she said quickly. "How much did you say the rent was?"

"Three hundred and seventy-five dollars a month."

Robin's mouth fell open. Most of the places C.C. had looked at were five hundred dollars or more. "We'll take it!" she cried.

Ian laughed. "I'll give you the landlord's number. But don't you think you ought to show it to C.C. first?"

As if in response to Ian's question, the doorbell rang. "I'll bet that's her," Robin said eagerly. "I'll be right back."

She jumped down the stairs three at a time and flung open the front door, crying, "C.C., hurry up. I've found us an apartment!"

C.C. opened her mouth to answer, but Robin grabbed her hand and started dragging her up the stairs. "It needs work," she said, "but it's cheap and it's got everything we—"

Robin stopped talking when she felt C.C.'s hand pulling against hers. Glancing behind her she saw that C.C. was looking up the stairs at something on the landing. "Hi, there," C.C. said softly, turning on her most alluring smile.

Robin followed C.C.'s gaze. Ian was standing on the landing, looking down at them. "Hi," Ian said, his eyes glazing over as he stared at C.C.'s black miniskirt and fishnet stockings.

C.C. tossed her hair over her shoulder and smiled seductively. "Are you going to be our new neighbor?"

Robin felt a cold chill pass through her. C.C. knows I like Ian, she thought jealously. Why is she flirting with him like that? Suddenly the idea of moving into an apartment above the *Rock Rag* offices seemed a lot less appealing. In fact, Robin told herself, moving anywhere with C.C. is probably a big mistake.

Still, it was a little late to back out now. She'd already gotten her parents' permission, not to mention a raise in her allowance to help cover her share of the rent. Besides, she told herself, I'm probably overreacting. C.C. likes to flirt, but she doesn't mean anything by it. After all, she's already got a boyfriend. Robin looked up at Ian. I just hope *he* knows that, she thought anxiously.

"Well, come on," C.C. said impatiently, giving Robin a gentle nudge, "where's this fantastic apartment? Are we going to see it or aren't we?"

"Oh, yeah," muttered Robin. "Come on up." She glanced up at Ian. He was leaning against the banister, and when she caught his eye, he smiled—a cute crooked little smile that made her feel weak all over. Reassured—at least a little bit—Robin smiled back and hurried up the stairs.

||||||||||||||||||||||||||||| *8*

The Townhouse was a small bar in the basement of an undistinguished brick building in Chelsea. Robin showed up a few minutes past nine o'clock and walked inside. Luckily the man at the door took her five dollars without carding her. Maybe it's my outfit, she thought with satisfaction. She was wearing black jeans with turquoise leg warmers and black ankle-high boots, plus a flannel black-and-turquoise plaid men's shirt with a black leather tie. She'd even taken the time to add some makeup (something she rarely bothered with) and pull one side of her curly hair away from her face with a tortoiseshell comb. All in all she thought she looked pretty mature, and she hoped Ian would be impressed.

All of the tables were taken, so Robin grabbed a stool at the bar and ordered a Perrier with lime. While she sipped it, she thought about her new apartment. Everything had happened so fast, it was hard to believe the place was really hers. Of course, it hadn't all been a piece of cake. C.C.'s first impression had been shock, followed immediately by total disgust. "I couldn't live here in a million years!" she'd shrieked when she walked into the living room. "It's filthy!"

But Robin and Ian had rhapsodized about the great location, the big, airy living room that was perfect for band rehearsals, and the amazingly low rent, and C.C.

had finally relented. "New York is one of the toughest places in the world to find an apartment—any apartment," Ian had told her. "We poor folk can't be too picky."

Ian was right, but Robin knew it was hard for C.C. to accept. After all, she was used to getting everything from her parents. Now, for the first time in her life, she was going to be on her own, earning her own money and paying her own bills—assuming she got it together and found a job, that is.

But Robin didn't want to think about that. Instead she returned to her memories of this afternoon. After C.C. agreed to rent the apartment, the girls had rushed uptown to the landlord's office. Luckily the apartment was still available, and after shelling out the first and last month's rent and another month's rent as a security deposit, they had signed the lease. As of February first the place would be theirs.

Robin and C.C. had left the landlord's office dancing with joy. After a celebration lunch at Life, the restaurant in their new neighborhood, they found a small student-size refrigerator in a secondhand shop on First Avenue and Ian helped them carry it upstairs.

The refrigerator brought Robin back to the money problem. C.C. had started out with $2000. They'd spent $210 on Gail's bass guitar, $1125 for the rent and security deposit, and $50 for the refrigerator. That left them with only $615—not exactly what you'd call big bucks.

Robin's calculations were mercifully cut short by the appearance of Naming of Parts. They walked onto the darkened stage unannounced and stood silently behind their instruments. When the crowd fell silent, the lights went up and the band broke into their first number.

Instantly Robin scanned the stage, looking for Ian.

He was standing behind a synthesizer, unmoving, his eyes glued on the keyboard, and a serious expression on his face. Robin thought his simple white shirt looked wonderful, and she loved the way one lock of hair hung down over his forehead and covered his left eye.

After she'd checked out Ian, she sat back and listened to the band. There were only two other guys onstage—another synthesizer player and a reed man. A drum machine beat out a loud, insistent rhythm, and the other instruments played odd, dissonant lines around it. At first Robin thought they were all improvising, but then she realized that every once in a while the parts came together in a sort of funky, Bach-influenced chorale.

Weird, Robin thought, definitely strange. Still, I kind of like it. She closed her eyes and sipped her drink. Just as she was getting used to the sound, someone started to sing—actually it was sort of a cross between talking and singing. Robin opened her eyes. It was Ian!

"Music," he recited in a singsong voice. "The art of combining sounds of various pitch to produce compositions expressive of various ideas and emotions. I said, music. A sequence of sounds produced according to this art. . . ."

Jeez! thought Robin. This is really far-out stuff. She was impressed, but a little annoyed too. It seemed no matter what she did, Ian was always one step beyond her. He was older than she, and while she was just moving out, he was already living away from home. She was working on *Rock Rag,* but he was the editor. She played in a rock band, but he played in an avant-garde combo.

When the song ended, the band immediately segued into their next number. The instruments played a repeating staccato pattern over a slightly cockeyed rhumba beat. "Those dirty stains!" Ian droned. "You've tried to soak them out, bleach them out, but you've still got . . . ring-around-the-collar!" Robin had to laugh. The lyrics were all well-known television commercials, and somehow the crazy rhumba music fit them perfectly.

The next song was deadly serious. Over minor chords and a haunting flute solo Ian intoned a poem describing the results of nuclear holocaust. After that it was back to comedy with a high-speed synthesized version of the theme from *The Tonight Show*. It went on like that through five more songs. The finale was a rock 'n' roll arrangement of the old kids' song that starts, "If you ever see a hearse go by, you know that you are the next to die. . . ."

The audience applauded enthusiastically as the band left the stage. This is a pretty hip crowd, Robin decided. At the Supermarket you either play danceable rock 'n' roll or you get booed off the stage. Mulling over the music she gulped down the last of her Perrier and ordered another. She was sucking on the ice when Ian sat down beside her.

"Hi!" he said with a grin. He ordered a beer and turned to her. "Well, out with it. What did you think?"

"I liked it," she said. "It was different. I like the way you sort of half talk, half sing the words."

"Thanks. Have you ever heard of Arnold Schoenberg? He was a Viennese composer who thought up a singing technique called *Sprechstimme*—speech-song. When I heard his stuff I thought, Hey, this would sound great combined with rock 'n' roll." He sipped his beer. "That's the whole basis of my music, really. I like to toss a little bit of everything into the pot—

classical music, rock, poetry, politics, kids' songs—stir 'em up, and see how it turns out."

"What does Naming of Parts mean?"

"It's the title of a poem by Henry Reed. It's great. I'll make a copy for you if you'd like to read it."

Arnold Schoenberg? Henry Reed? I never heard of either of those guys, Robin thought miserably. "I guess you must think Overnight Sensation is real kids' stuff compared to your band," she said flatly.

Ian looked puzzled. "Huh? What are you talking about?"

"Our music is just plain old rock 'n' roll. No poetry, no political statements, no artsy-fartsy speech-singing, or whatever it's called. Pretty boring, I guess."

"Is that the way I sounded?" He ran his hand through his hair and sighed. "Listen, sometimes I act like a real know-it-all. But I'm not, believe me. So I heard an Arnold Schoenberg record once. Big deal. My band isn't any better than Overnight Sensation. In fact, if you want to know the truth, I like your music better. All that hard-edged, up-tempo stuff—it's great. But I can't write songs like that. I tried, but it just sounded stupid." He shrugged. "So I learned to play the synthesizer and started writing the kind of stuff you heard tonight."

"Really?" she asked dubiously.

"Really." He reached out and laid his hand on her arm. "Robin, your music is really special." His dark-brown eyes were gazing intently into hers. "And I think you're pretty special too."

I was right, Robin thought wildly. He *does* like me. Every cell in her body seemed to be dancing for joy.

"Besides," Ian added, "what have you got to worry about? I'm still playing in little clubs like the Townhouse, but your band is getting ready to sign a deal with Backstage Records."

Robin swallowed hard. Why, oh, why did I have to go and lie about that? she asked herself. Okay, okay I know the answer. I wanted to impress him. But he's bound to find out the truth sooner or later, and then how impressed will he be?

Robin took a deep breath. "Uh, Ian," she began nervously, "about that Backstage Records deal, I, uh, I sort of stretched the truth a little. What I mean is, they're interested in us, but they didn't make any promises. Actually, they want to hear a demo first."

Ian smiled with one corner of his mouth and nodded knowingly. Oh, brother, Robin moaned silently, he probably thinks I'm a dope. "I'm sorry," she muttered, staring into her glass. "I guess I just wanted to impress you."

"Robin." Reluctantly she looked up. Ian was smiling for real now—that same five-hundred-watt smile he'd had on his face the first time they met. "You don't have to land a record deal to impress me. I was impressed the first time I laid eyes on you." He chuckled, remembering. "There you were onstage at the Supermarket, dancing around and singing those wimpy bubblegum songs. I looked at you and I thought, that girl is much too talented to be playing this kind of crap." He smiled. "And then, when you grabbed the microphone and tore into 'You Can't Stop Me Now'—man, I was just about blown away!"

"Really?" Robin asked, hardly daring to believe it was true.

He laughed. "Robin, if I didn't mean it, I wouldn't say it. Now, come on, let's get out of here. I'm starving and I have to get back in time to do another set at midnight." Throwing down some money he grabbed her hand and led her out of the club.

It was a damp, chilly night. The sky was filled with grayish-orange clouds and a few flakes of wet snow floated aimlessly to the ground. "There's an all-night diner just a few blocks from here," Ian said. "They make great potato pancakes. How's that sound?"

"By the highway? Oh, yeah, I've been there. It's great."

Ian took off down the street and Robin fell in beside him, easily matching his long, loping stride. "Hey," he said, smiling with pleasure, "you're the first girl I've ever walked with who could keep up with me. Usually I have to slow down."

Robin giggled. "Most boys think I walk like a giraffe."

"What do they know? A gazelle, maybe, but never a giraffe. Anyhow, I like it." He slipped his arm around her waist and they fell into step together.

The diner was a long, low building with chrome walls, a blue Formica counter, and Naugahyde booths. When the waitress came over, they ordered coffee and potato pancakes with sour cream.

"Have you lived in New York all your life?" Ian asked, tapping his fingers on the table in time to the music on the jukebox.

"I was born in New Jersey, in Trenton. My dad was at Princeton going for his doctorate. The next year he got a teaching job at NYU and we moved here. We've been in the city ever since." The waitress brought the coffee and Robin poured in some cream. "How about you? Where do you come from?"

"I grew up in Haverford, outside of Philadelphia. I went to Rutgers for a year, but I didn't like it. Everyone was into ZZ Top and Van Halen. No one had ever heard of musicians like Laurie Anderson, Phillip Glass, Robert Fripp . . . you know, innovators like that. So I dropped out and moved to New York to get in on the new music scene."

Robin had heard of those people, but she didn't

know much about them. Rather than show her ignorance she just nodded. Later, she told herself, when I get to know Ian better, I'll ask him all about his favorite musicians, maybe even borrow some of his records. But right now she had something more important on her mind. She waited until the waitress had brought the food. "Ian," she began, "remember when we first met . . ."

"Every second is indelibly etched on my brain." He grinned and shoved a forkful of food into his mouth.

"Good." She giggled. "But listen, you told me you'd produced demo tapes for a few local bands. And you said when Overnight Sensation was ready to record, you might be interested."

"Right. So?"

"Well, we're ready. That is, we will be, as soon as we raise the money. So, uh, what I want to know is, would you consider producing our demo?"

Ian didn't answer. Taking a bite of a pancake he stared pensively out the window for what seemed like an eternity. Then he turned to Robin and said, "First thing you need to know is, I won't accept a flat fee. I'll produce the tape for free and then if you get a record deal you can pay me back by letting me play on your album. Second, we have to talk to the other girls and see how they feel about the idea. I don't want to get involved unless the entire band is interested. If they agree . . . well, then, you've got yourself a producer."

"Oh, this is great!" she cried. "Thanks, Ian! You're terrific!"

"Hey, come on, you don't have to thank me. If this deal works out, it'll be good for both of us. Besides, I like your music." He reached across the table and took her hand. "And I like you."

Robin felt shaky and excited. She reached for her

coffee and almost knocked it over. Gulping down the hot liquid she gazed into Ian's face. Dark-brown eyes with the two little wrinkles in between, high cheekbones, a long straight nose, and a wide, expressive mouth. Just looking at him made her feel warm all over. "I like you, too, Ian," she said softly. "A lot."

"Then will you come back to the Townhouse and watch the band's next set? When we're done playing, I'll walk you home."

"Sure. That sounds great."

Ian sat back in the seat and stretched out his legs. "Hey, you know," he said, "what with you working for *Rock Rag* and me producing your demo tape, it looks like we're going to be seeing a lot of each other." He swallowed his last bite of potato pancake and shot her a wry smile. "Robin, I know you wouldn't want our feelings for each other to get in the way of our work. So, uh, if you think it would be best for us to keep our relationship strictly business, well, I'll understand."

Robin didn't stop to think it over. "No!" she cried. *"No way!"*

Ian laughed softly, then leaned across the table and kissed her lightly on the lips. "Robin," he said softly, "that's exactly what I was hoping you'd say."

|||||||||||||||||||||||||||| **9**

On the night of C.C.'s birthday Kurt arrived at her house wearing a blue beret. In his arms were a bouquet of yellow roses, a bottle of red wine, and a small package. "Happy birthday!" he announced when she opened the door. "You can't come to Paris with me, so I thought I'd bring a little bit of Paris to you."

C.C. smiled, but her heart wasn't in it. "When's your flight?" she asked.

"Tomorrow morning. Eight o'clock. Will you come see me off?"

"I can't. Robin and I are moving into our new apartment tomorrow. I'll be busy all day."

"Oh," he said, his face falling. "Well, be sure to give me your new address. I'll send you a postcard as soon as I get there and—"

"You don't have to," she interrupted. "I meant what I said that night at Touch. Just forget about me and have fun. When you get back, we'll pick up where we left off—if we're both still interested, that is."

Kurt frowned. "All right, if that's what you want. But that doesn't change how we feel about each other right now, does it?"

C.C. met his gaze. The blue beret gave him a rakish look, but his brown eyes were serious and intense. It would be better if we just broke up now, she told herself. Then I wouldn't be hurt later. But she couldn't bring herself to do it. Instead, she put her arms around his neck and kissed him.

"Hmm," he murmured, "I like the way you answered that question."

"Come on into the living room," she said, accepting the flowers. "I'll get some wineglasses."

"Kurt! How nice to see you!" Mrs. Collins walked shakily into the living room, a bottle of brandy dangling from her hand. Leaning against the back of the wing chair she looked around and asked vaguely, "Now, where do you suppose I put that glass?"

"Hello, Mrs. Collins," Kurt said politely. "How are you?"

"*I'm* just fine. I only wish I could say the same for Catherine. She's gotten some wild scheme into her head about moving out."

"It's not a wild scheme," C.C. said tersely, striding in from the dining room with the wineglasses. "It's reality. I'm moving out February first. Daddy said—"

"All your father cares about is saving money. If you move out that's just a few more dollars he can hand over to that . . . that gold digger!"

C.C. laughed uncomfortably. "Come on, Kurt. Let's go into my room."

"Try to talk some sense into her, Kurt, honey," Mrs. Collins called after them. "I know *you'd* never do anything to embarrass *your* family."

"Whew!" Kurt muttered as they stepped into C.C.'s room and closed the door. "Your mother is in pretty bad shape."

"I know." She put the wineglasses on the floor and flopped down on the bed. "Oh, Kurt, I feel so guilty. I keep worrying that maybe I'm doing the wrong thing."

Kurt sat down next to her and slipped his arm around her waist. "No, you're not. Hanging around here isn't going to solve your mother's problems. She has to do that herself."

"Well . . . she went to see a shrink last week. I guess that's a start."

"That's right. Besides, it's not as if you're leaving her completely alone. She's got lots of friends in Short Hills. And you can take the train out here anytime you want." He smiled and gave her a gentle squeeze. "Now, come on, birthday girl, open your present while I break out the wine."

"Oh, Kurt," she exclaimed impulsively, "what would I do without you?" But as soon as the words left her mouth, she wished she hadn't said them. Don't be ridiculous, C.C., she admonished herself. Tomorrow Kurt leaves for Europe and then you *will* be without him. You've got to accept that. You've got to forget about him and take care of yourself.

Kurt had produced a corkscrew from his pocket and was working on the wine bottle. "I have to admit, I'm glad to hear you say that," he said. "I was beginning to think you were happy to be getting rid of me."

C.C. didn't know what to say. Of course she didn't want to get rid of him. The problem was, after a month in London and Paris, maybe he'd want to get rid of her. Avoiding Kurt's eyes she picked up her present and tore off the wrapping. Inside she found a metallic, heart-shaped pendant on a silver chain.

"Do you like it?"

"Like it? I *love* it!" She examined the necklace more closely. The heart was red with black and silver hand-painted swirls. "Kurt, did you make this?" she asked in amazement.

"Yep." He poured the wine and handed her a glass. "Happy birthday, C.C.," he said softly. "From my heart to yours."

C.C. felt so full of love, she was sure she was going

to burst. She wanted to throw her arms around him and never let him go. I love you, Kurt, she said silently. I really do. But when she opened her mouth, all that came out was "Thank you."

Never mind, she told herself. It's better this way. Better to hold back a little, play it cool. That way I won't get hurt.

Kurt took her glass and put it down on the floor next to his. Picking up the necklace he opened the clasp and put it around her neck. The touch of his warm hands sent a shiver of pleasure down her spine. "I'm going to miss you, C.C.," he whispered in her ear.

Relax, C.C. told herself. Play it cool. She tried to laugh, but the sound died in her throat as Kurt took her face in his hands and kissed her. Closing her eyes she kissed him back, using her lips to say all the things she couldn't put into words.

Annette staggered up the stairs with a stack of records in her arms, a Raggedy Ann doll over one shoulder, and a lampshade on her head. The living room of Robin and C.C.'s new apartment was an obstacle course of furniture, boxes, and paint cans. Dropping her load she pushed aside a pile of clothes and sprawled on the floor.

Gail, Robin, and C.C. followed a second later, each carrying an armload of records. "That's it!" Robin announced, collapsing onto a pile of boxes. "We're done!"

The girls had spent the entire day working on the apartment. First they'd peeled off the loose wallpaper and scrubbed out the bathroom and the kitchen. Using the Quinns' vacuum cleaner they'd got most of the plaster dust off the floors. In the afternoon they were joined by Robin's parents, her brother Hank, and Ian.

While Mr. Quinn tightened the sagging door hinges and replaced the washers in the sink, the rest of them set to work painting the walls. When they were finished, the kitchen was a sunny yellow, the bedroom was sky-blue, the bathroom was shocking pink, and each of the living-room walls was a different color—blue, yellow, red, and green.

Robin glanced around the living room and smiled approvingly. The wild colors were her idea, but C.C. had readily agreed. They'd lived in tasteful off-white rooms all their lives. Now they were on their own and they could do whatever they wanted. Why not go a little nuts?

The rest of the day had been spent moving. Robin's parents went home and the girls drove Robin's orange Toyota out to Short Hills. Robin pursed her lips and frowned, remembering. Mrs. Collins had been waiting in the foyer, drunk and belligerent and refusing to let C.C. take her things. Reason wouldn't change her mind and neither would arguing, so finally they forgot about the furniture, the stereo, the books, and the records, and just grabbed C.C.'s clothes and toiletries and left as fast as they could.

Robin looked across the room at C.C. She was smoking a cigarette and staring pensively out the window. It's been a tough day for her, Robin thought sympathetically. She smiled gratefully, remembering how laid back and understanding her own parents had been. Not only had they given her some linens and the spare furniture they kept stored in the basement, they'd also come up with a mattress and pillow for C.C.

"Hey, C.C.," Robin exclaimed, hoping to cheer her up, "welcome to your new home!"

C.C. smiled grimly. "I'm just glad to be getting out

of Short Hills. From now on this apartment is my home and the band is my family."

"We're with you," Annette said earnestly. Gail and Robin nodded. For a long moment nobody spoke. It felt good just to be there together.

"Speaking of the band," Robin said, "I've got some big news." She stood up to face the girls and said eagerly, "I asked Ian if he'd produce our demo tape and he said yes! He's not going to charge us anything either. All he asked is that we let him play on our first album. Isn't that great?"

"Sounds wonderful!" C.C. replied, perking up.

"I'm not so sure about that," Annette said glumly. "We've already seen what happens when we let a guy tell us what to do."

"You mean Reg?" Robin asked. "But that was completely different. He was just using us to make a quick buck. Ian likes our music—and he likes us."

Gail cleared her throat. "You and Ian are going out together, aren't you Robin?"

Robin nodded. "I went to see his band play at the Townhouse last week. And this Saturday we're going to Danceteria. So?"

"Well, remember when C.C. started getting involved with Reg? You said it would cause problems and it did. Maybe boyfriends and business just don't mix."

"Hey, what's with you two?" Robin demanded. "C.C.'s not worried, are you, C.C.?"

"No, of course not," she replied. "Ian's a doll. I'd love to work with him."

Suddenly Robin remembered the sedutive way C.C. had smiled at Ian the afternoon he showed them the apartment. Quickly, she pushed the thought out of her mind and turned to Annette and Gail. "Look, I understand where you're coming from, but I don't think there's anything to worry about. Ian isn't trying to exploit us or anything like that. And he's not the kind of guy who plays favorites. Anyhow, where else can we find someone who'll produce us for free?"

"You've got a point there," Gail agreed.

"So what do you say? Let's give it a try. If it doesn't work out, we can always change our minds."

"Well . . . okay," Gail said with a nod.

Annette shrugged and searched her pockets for a piece of bubblegum. "Oh, all right. I guess so."

For a moment no one spoke. Then Gail said softly, "I found a job playing the piano at a restaurant in Newark. I start this weekend." She smiled. "And . . . and I met a boy. He works at the restaurant. His name is Flip."

"Hey, that's great!" Robin enthused. "Did he ask you out?"

"Oh, no," Gail answered bashfully. "We only just met. But he's awfully cute. And I'm going to see him at the restaurant Friday night."

"Way to go, Gail!" C.C. exclaimed. "Now we just need to find a boyfriend for Annette."

"No, thanks," she replied, popping a stick of gum into her mouth. "I'm happy just the way I am."

"But haven't you ever met a guy who turns you on?" C.C. asked.

"Sure, lots. But it takes more than looks to impress me. Most guys are only interested in themselves. When I find one who treats me as an equal, well, then, maybe I'll ask him out."

Robin laughed. "How romantic!"

"Well, maybe I don't spend all my time writing love songs like you do, but—"

"Hey, my songs aren't all love songs. What about 'You Can't Stop Me Now' or 'Overnight Sensation'?"

"They're great. But if I was a songwriter, I'd write

about really relevant stuff. You know, war and poverty and sexism—and what we can do to end them."

"So why don't you?" Robin asked.

"Oh, come on. You're the songwriter in this group, not me. Besides, I'm a drummer. You can't write music on the drums."

"So just write the words. I'll put them to music."

Annette sat up. "Are you serious?"

"Sure, why not? There's no law that says this band can only have one songwriter."

Annette nodded thoughtfully. "Well, who knows? Maybe I'll give it a try."

"Hello? Anybody home?" The girls looked up to see Ian peering around the door. "Boy!" he exclaimed, surveying the jumble of furniture and boxes. "This place looks like a hurricane hit it." He glanced at the girls and added, "And you four don't look too hot either."

"Gee, thanks," Robin said with a laugh. C.C., she noticed, quickly brushed the plaster dust off her shirt and straightened her hair. Just to be on the safe side Robin did the same.

"Just kidding." He lifted a box off one of the chairs and sat down. "Well, did Robin tell you I agreed to produce your demo? If you're interested, that is."

"Yes," Robin answered with more enthusiasm than honesty. "We're all really excited."

"Hey, that's great." He looked at each of the girls. "We've got a lot of things to talk about. Practice schedules, what songs we're going to record, arrangements, when you want to go into the studio . . . and, C.C.," he added almost as an afterthought, "unless you want to start sounding like Rod Stewart, I'd advise you to lay off the cigarettes."

C.C. looked surprised and a little annoyed, but Gail nodded and Annette said, "Good idea, C.C. You're voice has been sounding pretty scratchy lately." C.C. looked disgusted, but she threw her cigarette on the floor and ground it out with her heel.

Ian smiled approvingly. "Listen, whaddaya say I take you all out to dinner to celebrate our new musical partnership? Someplace really classy, like, say . . . McDonald's?"

"Yeah!" the girls cried, instantly alert. "Let's go! I'm starving!"

C.C., Annette, and Gail hurried out into the hallway, but Ian waited while Robin searched her pockets for her keys. "Robin," he said thoughtfully, "I want you to come up with some new songs for this demo. 'You Can't Stop Me Now' is okay, but if you want to be taken seriously, you'll have to come up with something a little more sophisticated."

"What's wrong with 'You Can't Stop Me Now'?" she asked defensively.

"Nothing. I just think you can do even better. Like I said in my review, there's no doubt in my mind you're going to be a star someday."

Ian turned on his Christmas-tree smile and Robin felt suddenly elated. Impetuously she stood on tiptoe to kiss his cheek, but Ian turned his head and their lips met, hesitantly at first, then eagerly in a deep, warm kiss.

||||||||||||||||||||||||| *10*

Gail's bus got caught in a traffic jam and it was almost eight o'clock by the time she got off in front of Bernard's for her first night of work. Avoiding the waitresses with their heavy trays of food, she walked quickly through the restaurant and into the Fishnet Lounge.

The lounge was crowded with customers. Every barstool was taken, every table was filled, and a few people were standing by the door. "I thought I told ya to be here at seven forty-five," Max said when he saw Gail.

"Yes, I'm sorry. My bus was late. It won't ha—"

"Spare me the excuses. Just get over there and play. We got a good crowd tonight and I wanna see 'em feeling happy and buyin' those drinks. Got the permit?"

"Yes, sir." Gail had gone to the Newark police station to be fingerprinted the day after she got the job.

"Okay. Gimme your stuff. I'll keep it back here. Now, get goin'."

Gail took her coat off and smoothed out the front of her silky peach-colored dress. With her head bowed she walked to the piano and sat down. Suddenly a woman with a mass of wavy blond hair tapped her roughly on the shoulder and said, "Play something pretty, kid."

Obediently Gail launched into the Olivia Newton-John song "Have You Never Been Mellow." So many people were smoking cigarettes that the piano was enveloped by a gray cloud. Gail cleared her throat and tried not to cough.

"Hey, hon," one of the men called, "how 'bout playin' 'Happy Birthday' for my sweetheart here?"

Gail obliged and the crowd started singing, loudly and off key. Bored, she closed her eyes and imagined she was playing with Overnight Sensation. Rock 'n' roll is much more fun than these middle-of-the-road pop tunes, she thought wistfully. In fact, Beethoven is a lot more fun too. She saw herself sitting at the baby grand at home, playing through one of the sonatas. They were all so beautiful. . . .

Gail's daydream was cut short when "Happy Birthday" ended and the people standing around the piano broke into a rowdy cheer. "How about 'A Bicycle Built For Two'?" someone called. Gail knew the basic melody, so she figured she could fake it. She started playing and the people around the piano sang along.

It went on like that for what seemed to Gail like an eternity. People left the lounge and others came in. Some drifted away from the piano and others drifted over. While she played, Gail kept her eye on the lounge entrance, hoping to spot Flip. So far, however, the only workers she'd seen were the waitresses who came into the bar to pick up their drink orders.

"Hey, kid," Max called. "Wanna take a break?" Gail nodded eagerly. "Go out to the kitchen," he told her. "And be back in fifteen minutes."

Gail left the lounge and walked back to the kitchen. The clock said ten o'clock. Two hours down and two to go. And the same thing again tomorrow night. Remember the money, she told herself. Thirty dollars a night. If I keep at it, pretty soon Overnight Sensation will have enough to start recording.

"Hey, sweet thing! What's up? Maxin' and relaxin'?"

Gail looked up and saw Flip standing there with his hands on his hips and a big grin on his face. "Hi, Flip," she said shyly. "I'm taking a break."

"I heard you playin'. You real good. But that music they got you doin' is strictly wack."

"Wack?"

"Yeah, you know. The pits!"

Gail laughed. "You're right. But it's what the people want to hear."

"Yeah, well, those fat cats don't know what's good." He rested his hand against the wall and leaned in close. "You live in Newark?"

She could feel his warm breath on her cheek. "N-No," she stammered. "Maplewood."

Flip took a step back and stared at her. "Maplewood? Are you jivin' me? There ain't no blacks out there."

Gail nodded. "Not many, anyway. My family used to live in The Bronx, but we moved to Maplewood last summer when my father got a job there."

"The Bronx, huh? You must be into hip-hop then, right?"

"There was lots of break-dancing and rapping going on, I guess, but I don't know much about it. My family is interested in classical music," she added. "My parents want me to apply to Juilliard, but I'm playing in a rock band now, so I plan to go part time."

"Classical music? A rock band?" Flip looked her over and shook his head. "You a pretty far-out chick, you know that, Gail?"

Gail felt her cheeks grow hot. Does he think I'm

strange? she wondered, surprised at how much that bothered her. "Well, I uh . . ."

"I'm not putting you down," he said quickly. "It's just that in my neighborhood it's the guys that are into music. Chicks mostly just hang around lookin' good. But you're different." He looked her over and nodded his head. "I like that."

"Thanks. Oh! My fifteen minute are up. I have to get back."

"Me too. Catch you later, baby." Flip shot her a dazzling smile and sauntered off through the swinging doors.

Back in the lounge Gail resumed her seat at the piano and played through the Barbara Streisand song "The Way We Were." Glancing around she noticed the atmosphere in the bar had changed. There were fewer middle-aged couples and more singles, especially men. The noise level was louder and the smoke was even thicker.

After a half hour or so a few men lurched over to the piano. They were in their thirties and from the sound of their uncontrolled laughter, Gail decided they must be drunk.

"Look at this," exclaimed one of them, a tall dark-haired man with a large diamond ring and a diamond tie clasp. "A new piano player!"

Gail smiled politely and kept on playing. "Let me buy you a drink, baby," the diamond man said. "Max!" he called, "gimme a highball over here!"

"No, thank you," Gail muttered, shaking her head.

An overweight man with pudgy white fingers leaned over the keyboard. Gail could smell the liquor on his breath as he asked, "Whatcha doing later tonight, sweetie? Ya wanna go out with me?"

The men laughed and Gail tried to smile too. Don't let them get to you, she told herself. They're just fooling around. She ran through a few verses of "Take Me Home, Country Roads," and to her great relief the men drifted off to the bar.

But a few minutes later they were back. "Max tells us you're just a kid," the guy with the diamonds said. "Seventeen years old." He laughed. "Sweet seventeen and never been kissed?"

Gail looked over to Max for help, but he was waiting on some customers on the other side of the bar. "Would you give *me* a kiss?" Pudgy Fingers asked.

The men were all around her and Gail felt so uncomfortable that she was playing all the wrong notes. Finally she stood up and made her way over to the bar. When Max noticed her, he frowned and asked gruffly, "What did ya stop playing for? You had yer break."

"Max, those men are embarrassing me," she answered shyly. "They keep asking me if I'll go out with them and if I've ever been kissed and things like that."

He shrugged and held out his hands, palm up. "Hey, kid, what can I tell ya? That's part of the scene. Flirt with 'em a little. Have some fun." He looked past her shoulder. "Oh, that's Eddie Pulanski and his friends. He drops a lot of dough here. Be nice to him, okay?"

"I—I'll try," she answered reluctantly. Making her way back to the piano she played through Billy Joel's "Just the Way You Are."

During the song Pudgy Fingers sidled up behind her and brushed lightly against her back. She moved forward, but a second later he was rubbing against her again. Turning around she looked up at him and said softly but firmly, "Please stop."

"Stop what?" he asked, all innocence.

Flustered, Gail turned back to the piano. Maybe she'd just imagined he was touching her. "Hey, sweetie," Eddie Pulanski said drunkenly. "Play a song for me. Do you know 'Brown Sugar'?"

"N-no," Gail muttered, hurrying through the last chorus.

He leaned over and grinned at her. "Brown sugar," he leered, "how come you taste so good?"

Gail felt like crying. Flirt a little, Max had told her. Have fun. But what was fun about listening to a bunch of obnoxious drunks make jokes at her expense? "Leave me alone!" she pleaded.

For a second she thought her words had had some effect. Eddie backed off and took a sip of his drink. Relieved, Gail continued playing. Then, abruptly, she felt something pressing against her back. Spinning around she saw Pudgy Fingers grinning down at her. "Don't stop," he muttered lasciviously. "When you run your hands over those keys it turns me on."

Gail was so shocked, she didn't know what to say. A feeling of panic was rising in her chest. All she could think was, I've got to get out of here. Avoiding the men's eyes she stood up and pulled down the cover on the keyboard. It dropped with a crash, and a few customers looked over at her in surprise. "Hey, sweetheart," Pudgy Fingers asked innocently, reaching out to fondle her shoulder, "what's the matter with you?"

"Don't touch me!" she cried, frantically pushing his hand away. Hot tears blurred her vision. "Just leave me alone!"

"Hey!" Max yelled. "What the hell's goin' on? Gail, sit down and play."

"Hear that, brown sugar?" Eddie muttered under his breath. "The boss wants you to keep playing."

Impetuously Gail spun around and slapped Eddie on the cheek. Startled, he stepped back and blinked at her. For a long moment no one moved.

Then, suddenly, everyone turned to look at the entrance that led to the restaurant. Gail turned, too, and to her amazement she saw Flip making his way through the crowd. His stride was quick and powerful and his white busboy's uniform seemed to glow in the dim light of the lounge. Coming up beside her he put his arm protectively around her shoulders and said loudly, "Leave my woman alone!"

"Your woman, huh?" Pudgy Fingers jeered. "Well, don't worry, boy. We just wanna borrow her for the ni—"

Before the words had left the man's lips, Flip spun around and shoved his palm into the fat man's chest. Pudgy Fingers fell back and slammed against the piano. Instantly Eddie ran at Flip with both fists in the air. Flip ducked, but Eddie's knuckle still caught him in the cheek.

"All right!" Max yelled, running out from behind the bar. "Break it up! Break it up! He grabbed one of Flip's arms and bent it roughly behind his back. "Just what do you think you're doing?" he asked tersely, glaring at Gail. Without waiting for a reply he turned to Eddie and his friends. "I'm very sorry, Mr. Pulanski. I'll make certain this kind of thing never happens again."

"But, Max—" Gail began.

"I should have known better than to hire someone like you," he said with disgust. "You're fired." He pushed Flip toward the door. "You, too, wise guy. Now, get out of here. Both of you."

Gail pressed her tongue against the roof of her mouth to hold back the tears. Everyone was staring at her, but she refused to let them see how much they'd hurt her. Silently, with her head held high, she followed Flip through the lounge, pausing only to collect her coat and purse from behind the bar.

In the kitchen Flip squeezed her shoulder and said quietly, "Hang tight. I just gotta change."

Leaning against the wall she took a Kleenex from her purse and blew her nose. A minute later Flip returned. He was wearing a black hooded sweatshirt, a brown leather bomber jacket, jeans, and loosely laced Pro-Keds. Offering his arm he said loudly, "Come on, baby. Let's split."

Gratefully Gail took his arm, and together they walked out into the darkness. "Flip," she began, when the door had closed behind them, "I—I feel terrible. I mean, you lost your job and it's all because of me. You didn't have to get involved, but . . . well, what I mean is . . . I'm really sorry."

"Listen, don't apologize. I've been dyin' to punch out one of those guys ever since I started workin' there. They think they're so goddamned superior."

"But what about your job? I mean, can you find another?"

"No problem. I'm makin' more money break-dancin' on the street anyhow. I'm in a crew—Fresh Body Rockers. We dance downtown and in the city. We're the baddest breakers in Newark," he said with obvious pride. "No contest."

"Well, uh, thanks for helping me out," she told him, turning to go.

Flip grabbed her arm. "Hey, chill out. Where you off to in such a hurry?"

"I have to get home. My parents are expecting me."

"Forget about that. Let's go over to the All-City Club. They got some fresh music and everybody be dancin'. My crew's over there and you can see us in action, rockin' the place."

"I—I can't," she said. Her parents thought she was in the city practicing with Overnight Sensation. If she didn't get home by twelve-thirty, they'd be suspicious, not to mention terrifically upset. "Maybe some other time."

"Okay, how about tomorrow night? We can meet in the city and check out the Roxy."

Gail looked at Flip. A single spotlight shining down from the roof of Bernard's threw his face into sharp relief. In his tight jeans and bomber jacket he looked tough and dangerous—just the type of boy her parents had warned her to stay away from back when they lived in The Bronx. In the past Gail had always agreed with them. She didn't like the street kids with their sullen expressions, their tough talk, and their wild clothes. Her fantasies always centered around her piano teacher, Mr. Dawson. Now, *that* was the kind of man for her. Handsome, cultured, well dressed, well spoken. . . .

"I can't go," she said, shaking her head. "Thanks, but . . . well, I just can't."

Flip released her arm and shot her a scornful look. "Okay, I get it. You think I'm not your type. That's cool. Just go on back to Maplewood, then, and see how far you get with those rich white boys."

No, Gail wanted to say. I don't know anyone in Maplewood. They're not my friends. But Flip was already walking into the shadows. "Flip—" she called.

His voice came to her from out of the darkness. "If you change your mind you can find me at the All-City Club." His voice was proud and strong. "Ask anyone. They all know who I am."

Gail heard a rustling in the darkness, and then he was gone. "Did I do the right thing?" she whispered, looking up at the stars. But no answer came to her. All she knew was that she was confused. Confused and unhappy and tired—oh, so tired. Forget him, Gail, she told herself. Forget Bernard's. This whole ridiculous job has been a mistake from beginning to end. Better to just put it out of my mind and concentrate on important things—like Overnight Sensation. Holding that thought in her mind she turned her back on the restaurant and hurried across the parking lot to the bus stop.

‖‖‖‖‖‖‖‖‖‖‖‖‖‖‖‖‖ *11*

"Eeee! Oh, yuck! *Disgusting!*" C.C. came running into the living room, frantically pulling her pale-blue bath robe over her shoulders. "Robin," she moaned, "I can't stand this anymore!"

Robin was sitting on the floor with her electric guitar in her lap and a pad and pencil in front of her, working on a new song. "What is it now?" she asked, not looking up.

"Roaches! Oh, Robin, it's too gross. I got in the shower and there were two of them on the curtain. Then when I pushed the curtain back to jump out, one of them fell on my shoulder." She shuddered, remembering. "Right *on* me. I mean, the creature actually touched my flesh!"

Robin nodded distractedly. Roaches didn't bother her the way they bothered C.C. Besides, she was trying to come up with a rhyme for the word *room*. Gloom, broom, tomb . . .

"Robin!" C.C. shrieked. "You aren't even listening to me!"

With a disgusted grunt Robin set down her guitar

and stared at her new roommate. "Look, what do you want me to do? We already bought a bunch of roach motels. The only other solution is to have the place exterminated, and you know we can't afford that."

"Oh, man," C.C. muttered, shaking her head. "Just listen to you. All you ever talk about these days is money." Pulling her robe around her she padded across the living room and flopped down on the sofa—a ratty red velvet monstrosity Robin had found on the street. "This place is a dump. A slum!" C.C. paused significantly. "But it has potential. Now, if we just hired someone to remodel the kitchen, and sand the floors and . . ."

C.C. chattered on, eagerly describing how they could turn the apartment into an *Architectural Digest* cover story. Wearily Robin rubbed her eyes. C.C.'s right, she thought. This place *is* a dump. The sinks are clogged, two of the burners on the stove don't work, and the radiators barely produce enough heat to get the temperature up to sixty. But at least it's cheap. "Look, C.C.," she said irritably, "if you don't like it here, you can always move back in with your mom. Or better yet, get a job."

"I'll never move back to Short Hills," she answered indignantly. "And as for the job, I'm trying. I've been in every boutique and art gallery in lower Manhattan, but so far nothing has worked out."

"Yeah, well, maybe it's time you forgot about the art galleries and applied for some regular jobs—like waitress or secretary or something."

"Come off it," C.C. scoffed. "You didn't want a job like that and neither do I. Besides, once Overnight Sensation makes that demo tape, we won't have to worry about money anymore."

"Well, maybe . . ." Robin prided herself on being realistic about the band's chances, but even she had to admit that things were going well. Since Ian became their producer, Overnight Sensation had been practicing four nights a week, and they were really starting to sound tight. Robin was writing some new songs, and under Ian's firm guidance, C.C. had cut her smoking down from a pack a day to couple of packs a week.

As if on cue C.C. picked up a pack of cigarettes from the end table, paused a moment, then dropped them. "When are we going to start recording?" she asked.

"Soon," Robin answered. But for a change her mind wasn't on the demo tape. She was thinking about C.C. and the way she'd been flirting with Ian. Ever since that first day he'd shown them the apartment, she'd been playing up to him. Nothing too obvious—hardly worth mentioning, really—but little things, like smiling a little too sweetly or staring at him just a little too long. "Hey, C.C.," Robin said nonchalantly, "how's Kurt? I've noticed you haven't mentioned him for a while."

"Kurt? Oh, he's in Europe with his father. He won't be back for a month, at least."

"Europe? I can't believe you didn't mention it! When did he leave?"

"Just before we moved in here."

"Poor C.C.," Robin said sympathetically. "You must miss him."

C.C. shrugged. "Not really. We like each other, but neither of us is ready for a serious commitment. If he goes out with someone while he's over there, that's okay. And if I find someone else, that's okay too." She reached for the pack of cigarettes again, but this time she took one out and lit it. Inhaling deeply, she added, "Maybe it's time I moved on to someone new. Kurt is nice, but he's a little too Short Hills for my taste. I need a city boy. Someone who's into the rock scene, you know?"

So that's it, Robin thought angrily. Kurt's getting boring so it's time to move on to someone new. Someone like Ian Harkin. Well, forget it, C.C. Ian is mine. "Look," she said tersely, "I'm trying to write this song. Why don't you go take your shower so I can concentrate?"

"All right," C.C. answered. "Don't get so uptight. I was just leaving."

"Good. And while you're in there, you can figure out what we're going to eat for dinner. All we've got in the refrigerator is a bottle of ketchup and some three-day-old tuna fish."

"Maybe we could go over to your parents' place."

"Forget it. We've eaten over there twice this week. That's enough." Robin stretched out her long legs and sighed. "Look, C.C., I know moving in here hasn't been all that easy for you. I mean, this isn't exactly the lap of luxury, you know?"

C.C. rolled her eyes. "Tell me about it."

"Yeah, yeah. And I know I'm better off financially too. I've got an allowance, for one thing. But don't forget, I've also got a job."

"Okay, I'm impressed." C.C. puffed her cigarette thoughtfully. "Robin, I'll tell you what. Tomorrow I'll hit some of the uptown boutiques and galleries. If I can't find a job . . . I don't know, maybe I'll have to use my last resort."

"Last resort? What do you mean?"

"We-ell . . . in Kurt's last letter he told me I could have a job at his father's law office if I needed it. All I have to do is go in there and he said he'd take care of the rest. It would just be filing and answering the phone—real Mickey Mouse stuff—but I *guess* I could take it."

Robin jumped up and shook C.C. by the shoulders.
"You dodo! Why didn't you tell me about this before?"

"Because. I don't want to work at some boring nine-
to-five job. Besides, Kurt and I are probably breaking
up. I don't want him doing me any favors, you know?"

"I don't care if you loathe each other. Unless you
want to start eating roach stew for dinner, you better
take that job."

"Oh, yuck! I think I'm going to be sick!"

"Fine. Just go do it in some other room. Before I
was so rudely interrupted, I was hard at work writing
the band's first number-one song."

"Ex*cuse* me!" With a long-suffering sigh C.C.
walked off to the bathroom and Robin went back to
her songwriting.

"Let's see," she muttered, chewing thoughtfully on
her pencil. "Room, loom, womb, zoom . . ."

Gail stepped off the bus and stood in the middle of
the sidewalk, staring at the graffiti-covered building
that housed the All-City Club. As she stood there, a
group of teenage boys strolled down the street. When
they reached the front of the club, one boy pulled a
bottle of wine out of his jacket. After passing it around
they tossed the empty bottle into the gutter and
walked inside. When the door opened, loud music
spilled out into the street and Gail could make out the
crush of bodies inside.

What am I doing! she asked herself, turning her
back on the club. I don't belong here. This is just the
kind of place my parents used to warn me about.
"Drinking, drugs, and fighting. That's what goes on in
places like that," her father had often told her. "I
won't have my family involved in that world. We're
going to make something of ourselves."

But that's what my parents said about rock 'n' roll,

too, Gail reminded herself, and look how wrong they were. Besides, it wasn't the music she was there for. It was Flip. Ever since that night at Bernard's she'd been thinking about him. The way he walked right into the bar and stood up to the men who were bothering her. The way he told them, "Leave my woman alone!" And the way he leaned close to her, so close that she could feel his warm breath on her cheek.

Hesitantly Gail crossed the street and stood in front of the club. Go on in, she urged herself. No one's going to hurt you.

"Right," she whispered, walking down the cement steps and pulling open the heavy door. Instantly the bone-crushing volume of the music assaulted her and she drew back against the wall, squinting uncertainly into the shadowy darkness.

The club was one large room with graffiti-covered walls and a low ceiling. In the far corner a DJ stood behind a long table, spinning records on two turntables. The dance floor was crowded with kids, moving in time to the music. Most of them, Gail noticed, were black, and all of them were dressed in hip-hop fashions—sweatsuits, tight jeans, leather and chains, and of course, sneakers. Gail looked down at her purple sweatshirt, jeans, and jogging shoes and hoped she fit in.

Suddenly the music stopped, then started again, louder than ever. Everybody looked up as the DJ started to rap.

"Now that I got everybody's attention,
I'm gonna let you in on a rockin' intention.
The Fresh Body Rockers gonna boogie and break,
Then ya'll can join in if you got what it takes."

Gail gasped. The Fresh Body Rockers! That was Flip's crew. The crowd had formed a large circle and now four boys in matching white sweatshirts and white baseball caps stepped into the center and started to dance. The tallest one had to be . . . yes, it was Flip!

With her heart pounding Gail joined the crowd and worked her way to the inside of the circle. One of the boys was dancing by himself now, moving his body like a robot in time to the music. And there on the other side of the circle was Flip, looking handsome and muscular in his sleeveless white sweatshirt and tight black jeans. "Go, Bop Boy!" Gail heard him shout. "Rock the joint!"

When Bop Boy was finished, the other two members of the crew had their turn. Finally, when it seemed as if the crowd had been treated to every dance step imaginable, Flip jumped into the circle. Dropping to the floor he pulled off a series of gravity-defying acrobatic moves. With only one hand to support him he stretched out parallel to the floor and rotated his body like an airplane propeller. Rolling over, he spun on his back, then leapt up and did a series of head-over-heels flips.

"Go, Flip-Flop!" his crew members yelled. "Do it, man!"

Flip responded with a head spin and climaxed with a no-hands shoulder spin. Gail just stared, awestruck. She'd never seen anybody dance like that. Flip's moves were athletic yet graceful, powerful but at the same time almost balletic. "Flip," she whispered with amazement, "you're beautiful!"

"He's in his power!" someone in the crowd yelled. "Awesome!"

"Hurray for Flip!" Gail cried, overcome with enthusiasm. The boy next to her threw her a disapproving frown. "I mean, *awesome!*" she amended with a bashful smile.

Flip jumped to his feet and strolled to the edge of the circle with his clenched fist in the air. As the crowd cheered, a newcomer moved into the center of the circle, hoping to prove that he was as good as the Fresh Body Rockers. But Gail didn't want to watch anyone else. Keeping her eye on Flip she edged her way around the circle until she was almost beside him. He was standing with his friends, watching the dancers and shouting put-downs. "Give up, boys!" he yelled. "The Fresh Body Rockers are gonna take you out!"

"Flip!" she called over the music. *"Flip!"*

Flip turned around, a look of irritation on his handsome face. But when he saw who it was, his expression changed from irritation to pleasure. "Welcome, Miss Gail," he said seriously, taking her hand and kissing it softly. "To what do I owe the honor of this visit?"

Gail stared up at him, tongue tied. She didn't know what to say, especially here in the middle of a crowded, noisy dance floor. "I—" she began. "I don't—"

Smiling, Flip put his arm around her. "Come on," he said. "Let's go somewhere we can talk."

"Hey, Flip, my man!" one of his friends yelled. "Where you goin'? We got business to attend to!"

But Flip just waved him away. Taking Gail's hand he led her across the club and out the door to the street. After being inside, the city street seemed silent as a church. Dropping her hand Flip looked at Gail and grinned. "So, little lady," he said in the no-nonsense voice of a TV-show cop, "looks like we meet again."

Gail laughed. Then, seriously, she said, "Flip, I'm sorry I acted so rude outside Bernard's. I was just upset, and . . . to tell you the truth, I . . . I was a little scared of you."

"Scared of me?" he asked curiously. "After I'd just lost my job trying to help you out?"

"I know it's silly, but . . . well, my life has been a little . . . sheltered, I guess you'd call it. The only boys I've ever known were classical musicians. They didn't talk like you, or dress like you." She smiled shyly. "And they couldn't dance like you either."

"Hey," he retorted, *"nobody* dances like me!" Then he shrugged and said, "I come on real cool, but deep down I'm not so tough. What I mean is, you don't have to be scared of me, Miss Gail. I like you—you know what I'm sayin'?"

Gail nodded. "I—I like you too," she said softly.

"Then what are we waitin' for? Let's get back in there and boogie." He turned and started for the door.

But Gail held back. "I can't dance like those kids in there," she muttered. "I—I can't dance at all."

Flip turned around and smiled at her. "Hey, everybody gotta start someplace, right? Look, here's a simple two-step to get you going." He snapped his fingers in a slow, steady beat and began to move. First he crossed his arms and put his right foot forward. Then, uncrossing his arms, he moved his right foot behind him and crossed his left leg in front. "Go on," Flip urged. "Try it."

"Well . . ." Hesitantly at first, then with a bit more confidence, Gail imitated Flip's moves. "Hey," she exclaimed, "this isn't so tough!"

Grinning, Flip moonwalked around Gail, rapping as he went.

"Take a look at this girl, her name's Miss Gail,
When she starts to boogie she just can't fail.
When she's by my side I feel so right,
I wanna keep on breakin' till the morning light.
So come on, girl, I won't do you no harm,

*I'm gonna show you some fun, I'm gonna turn
    on the charm.
'Cause when you learn how to dance you won't
    wanna stop.
Come on, Miss Gail, I'm gonna show you how to
    rock!"*

Gail started to giggle, and the next thing she knew,
her right leg was wrapped around her left and she was
tumbling to ground. Instantly Flip was there. Extending a hand he helped her to her feet and brushed
the dirt off her jeans. "You okay?"

"Sure. I just need a little more practice, that's all."

"Well, then, let's go inside. I'll teach you everything
you need to know." He doffed his baseball cap and
bowed from the waist. "I'd be honored to have you
with me, Miss Gail."

Gail giggled with pleasure. With a curtsy and a
smile she replied, "At your service, m'lord." Grinning,
he offered his arm. Gail took it, and they walked back
into the All-City Club together.

||||||||||||||||||||||||| **12**

By the end of February, Overnight Sensation had finally saved up enough money to record a demo.
Ground Sound, the studio where Ian had booked time,
was in the basement of an East Village dry cleaners.
One look told you it wasn't a high-rent operation—

exposed pipes leaked rusty water onto a stained red rug, and Gail swore she saw a mouse scurry across floor near Annette's bass drum—but Ian said the place had good acoustics and excellent eight-track equipment. Besides, considering how little money the girls had to spend, they couldn't afford to be choosy.

The band went into Ground Sound on the first Saturday in March. All those nights of rehearsing had obviously paid off, because after an initial moment of nervousness, they whipped through the songs without so much as a flubbed note. Ian recorded them live, just as if they were playing a concert, then overdubbed background vocals, extra percussion (like handclaps and tambourine), and Gail's piano parts. He even added some synthesizer lines himself.

After five hours of recording, the band had four songs on tape. The first was "Overnight Sensation," the song Robin had written when the band got back together. The second was a medium-tempo love song called "The Time of My Life." Next came "In My Rainbow Room," a dreamy psychedelic-influenced ballad Robin had written while watching the sun make patterns on the brightly colored walls of her apartment. Ian wanted to end the tape with a bang, so they finished up with "Lonely Girls"—three minutes of high-intensity rock 'n' roll that he said was guaranteed to make record-company executives sit up and take notice.

When the actual recording was over, the eight-track tape was mixed, edited, and transferred onto cassettes. Then Robin went to work. Over the next few days she took the cassettes—along with a brief cover letter, a biography of the band, and a publicity photo (taken by Robin's father)—around to every record-company office in Manhattan. In most cases a bored receptionist took the tape and told her, "We'll get back to you."

When Robin asked to see someone in the A&R (Artists and Repertoire) Department, the response was a polite but firm "No one's available right now. Call in a month if you don't hear from us."

Robin's last stop was Backstage Records. Despite the other companies' lack of hospitality she was almost certain she would get past the front desk there. After all, she reminded herself, Mr. Kaplan likes our music. When he finds out we made a tape, he'll probably want to hear it right away.

"Ben Kaplan told me to come in when I had a demo," she told the receptionist, a young woman with orange hair and a vapid expression. The nameplate on her desk said she was Miss Prist.

"Hmm," she muttered, reaching for the manila envelope Robin was holding. "I'll put it in his box."

Robin clutched the envelope to her chest. "Um, I'd rather give it to Mr. Kaplan in person. Is he in?"

Miss Prist tapped her pencil against the desk. "He's busy. Just leave the tape and he'll get back to you."

"But he said he wanted to see me in person," she lied.

"Do you have an appointment?"

"Well, no, but . . . That is, I thought . . ."

With a bored sigh Miss Prist picked up the phone and dialed three numbers. "Mr. Kaplan, there's a teenage girl here to see you."

"Robin Quinn," Robin whispered urgently. "Overnight Sensation. He saw us at the Supermarket last—"

"Quinn," she said into the phone. "The band's called Overnight Vacation. Says you wanted to see her . . . no, she doesn't have an appointment. . . . Yes, Mr. Kaplan. Yes, I'll tell her. Thank you." She hung up the phone and shot Robin a self-satisfied smile. "Mr. Kaplan doesn't remember you, but if you'll just leave the tape with me . . ."

Robin felt like crying, but determined not to show defeat, she threw her shoulders back and fixed her face in what she hoped was an expression of bored superiority. "Look, sweetie," she said haughtily, "Warner Bros. just offered us a four-album deal, and RCA is talking six figures, so you can tell Kaplan that if he doesn't get back to me by the end of the week, the deal is off. Got that? O-F-F. *Off!*" Tossing the cassette on the desk Robin turned her back on the stunned receptionist and strolled out the door.

During the next month Robin called the record companies once a week to ask about the Overnight Sensation demo. The typical response was a brusque "We'll get back to you" or "You'll be hearing from us through the mail."

By the second week the receptionist at Backstage Records had learned to recognize her voice. As soon as Robin said, "May I speak to—" the receptionist would drone, "Mr. Kaplan is busy. I'll tell him you called." Before Robin could get in another word, she'd hang up. And Ben Kaplan never called back.

To keep their minds off the demo the girls played some gigs at the Supermarket, the East Village club where they had once performed as C.C. and the Seniors. Other than that, they didn't spend much time together. Annette was spending most of her spare time writing song lyrics, although she hadn't gotten up the nerve to show them to anyone yet. Gail's parent still thought she was spending her weekend nights with Overnight Sensation, but the girls knew she was over in Newark, dancing at the All-City Club with Flip.

Meanwhile, C.C. was going out with a different boy almost every night of the week. When Robin asked about it, she laughed and said, "Oh, Kurt called to say he's spending another few weeks in Europe. He and his father are staying with some member of Parliament or something in London. All he could talk about was the guy's teenage daughter and how much fun they're having going to all the museums together." She tossed her hair over her shoulder and shrugged. "It's over, Robin. He's having a great time without me. Why shouldn't I have a great time too?"

Robin was dubious, expecially when C.C. started staying out all night, but she kept her mouth shut. She was out of the apartment a lot herself, either going to classes at NYU, selling ads and reviewing concerts for *Rock Rag*, or just hanging out at Ian's apartment, talking and listening to records.

Then one Friday near the end of March, Robin came home after an afternoon in the NYU library to find Annette waiting for her on the front steps. "Hey, hi there!" Robin greeted her. "What's up?"

Annette was chewing her gum even more furiously than usual. "I've been working on some lyrics. They're probably not very good, but, uh, you said you'd look at them when I finished, and so, well, here I am."

"Hey, that's great! Come on up." Robin unlocked the front door and picked up the mail. She glanced at it, then did a double take. "Annette! We got something!" Frantically she ripped open the first envelope. "It's from Polygram. *Dear Ms. Quinn, Thank you for giving us a chance to listen to your tape. Unfortunately . . .*" Robin's face fell and her voice went flat. *"Unfortunately it does not meet our needs at this time."*

"Morons," Annette muttered. "What do they know?"

Robin opened the next envelope. *"Dear Musician, Thank you for submitting your music for our consideration. However . . ."* She crumpled the letter in her hand. "Forget it. Epic isn't interested in us either."

"Oh, man! They must be tone deaf or something."

"Oh, well," sighed Robin. "Let's go upstairs and drown our sorrows in chocolate chip cookies."

"Now you're talking."

Robin stuck the letter in her notebook and they plodded up the stairs together. When they reached the landing, she stopped dead in her tracks. "The door's wide open," she whispered.

"So? Maybe C.C. opened it."

"No way. This is New York. We always keep it closed and locked, even when we're home. Wait here." She tiptoed across the landing and peeked around the open door. C.C. was standing in the middle of the living room, her arms draped around Ian's waist and her head on his shoulder. Robin closed her eyes and tried to ignore the sick feeling in the pit of her stomach. So, she thought miserably, all that flirting finally paid off. Well, thanks a lot, C.C. I hope you're happy.

She was still standing there when Annette came up behind her and threw open the door. "Robin, what's going on? I mean . . . oh!"

At the sound of Annette's voice Ian and C.C. turned toward the door. "Come on in!" C.C. bellowed. She pulled away from Ian and staggered toward them. In her hand was an empty wineglass. "We're having a party, just sweet little Ian and me!"

"I heard some weird noises, so I came up to make sure everything was okay," Ian explained. "Looks like she put away most of a bottle of tequila. I've been trying to get her to lie down, but it isn't easy."

Robin was so relieved, she felt like laughing. Instead she went over to C.C. and took hold of each arm. Looking her in the eye she said firmly, "What's going on?"

"I'm celebrating!" C.C. exclaimed. "I quit my job today. No more typing and filing. No more answering the phone. No more—"

"Quit your job? What are you, nuts? We need that money to pay the rent!"

"I don't care!" she cried. "Kurt's coming home this week and there's no way I'm going to work in that office while *he's* there." She shook her head dramatically. "I never want to see him again!" Then, suddenly, she threw down her wineglass and started to cry. "Oh, Christ, why don't you all just leave me alone?"

Ian grabbed her around her waist and led her over to the sofa. She fell across it and sobbed into her hands. "I'm just a drunk, no better than my mother. No wonder no one like me."

Annette knelt beside her and took her hand. "C.C., don't be silly," she said softly. "We all love you. And I'll bet Kurt does too."

"Not a chance. He's in love with some English girl."

"You don't know that," Robin told her. "Besides, I thought you said you weren't ready for a serious commitment. You told me you were both going to date other people while he was away."

"I just didn't want to get hurt," she muttered, wiping her nose with the back of her hand. "But it hurts anyway." She put her hand over her stomach and swallowed hard. "Annette," she moaned, "I think I'm going to be sick!"

"Oh, brother!" Forcing her arm under C.C.'s shoulders Annette helped her up and half walked, half dragged her down the hall to the bathroom.

Alone in the living room Robin and Ian looked at each other. "She'll be okay once she gets some of that tequila out of her system," Ian said. "Just put her to bed and let her sleep it off."

Robin nodded wearily. "I just opened two record-company rejections. And now this." She smiled weakly. "I guess this just isn't my day."

"Poor Robin." He held out his arms. "Come here."

Gratefully she accepted a hug. "When I looked in here and saw C.C.'s arms around you," she whispered, "I didn't know what to think. I—I was so afraid that you and she . . ."

"No way," he said firmly. "C.C.'s not my type. Besides, I don't want to be with anyone else. Just you." He gazed deep into her eyes, then leaned down and kissed her—a soft, slow kiss that made her tremble with pleasure.

The sound of retching from the bathroom put an abrupt end to the romantic moment. "Uh, maybe I better go help Annette," Robin said reluctantly.

Ian smiled. "You're a true friend. Look, I'm going downstairs to work on some album reviews. Come down later and we'll go over to my place for a nice romantic dinner."

Robin shot him a skeptical glance. "Last time you invited me over for dinner we had peanut butter and jelly sandwiches."

"Well, don't worry, I'm out of peanut butter. I thought maybe some nice cereal. I've got Wheaties and Raisin Bran and—"

"What a gourmet!"

Ian favored her with one of his five-hundred-watt smiles and she felt her knees go weak. When he looked at her like that, anything seemed possible—even a record contract from Backstage Records. "Okay," she said with an affectionate smile. "I'll be down in a few minutes." She gave him a quick kiss, then hurried down the hall to take care of C.C.

||||||||||||||||||| **13**

C.C. poured herself some coffee and read over Kurt's postcard one more time. *I'll be coming into Newark Airport April first at four-fifteen* P.M. *Can you come meet me? I really need to talk to you. Love, Kurt.*

C.C. shook her head. No way, she thought. I mean, why should I? I already know what he's going to say. "I met a girl in England and we fell in love. I hope you and I can still be friends but . . ."

She ripped the postcard in two and tossed it into the trash. Turning on her heel she opened the refrigerator and peered inside. A can of Tab, a bottle of ketchup, and a half-eaten Italian sub. Time to start looking for another job, she thought wearily. But no more supermarkets. She'd already quit a job at the local A&P when they told her she couldn't smoke behind the cash register. And no more clothing stores either. The Limited had dumped her just because she told some old lady that leather pants would make her look like a pregnant cow.

Well, it was true, C.C. thought indignantly. Unwrapping the sub she held her nose and took a bite. What's on for tonight? she wondered. Oh, yeah, I'm going to a party with that guy I met at Danceteria. What's his name? Robert . . . Roger, something like that.

The phone rang and she walked into the living room to answer it. "Hello?"

A male voice. "Robin Quinn, please."

C.C.'s law-office training was still with her. "She's not in right now. May I take a message?"

"Yes, please. This is Ben Kaplan from Backstage Records. Can you ha—"

"Backstage Records! Oh, wow! I mean, hi, there. Um, I'm C.C. From Overnight Sensation. The lead singer, you know, and uh, anything you want to tell Robin, you can tell me."

"Well," he said with a chuckle, "hello, C.C. Tell Robin I listened to that demo tape she brought over last month and I was very impressed. So impressed, in fact, that I caught one of your shows at the Supermarket, and . . . well, to make a long story short, I'd like the four of you to come up to my office tomorrow to discuss a contract."

"A contract?" C.C. gasped. "Like a record contract? I mean, you want us to make records?"

"That's the general idea. Are you under contract to anyone else at the moment?"

"No! I mean," she amended, trying desperately keeping her cool, "a few companies might be interested, but, you know, nothing *firm.*"

"Good. Well, I'll see the four of you with your manager tomorrow. Let's say eleven o'clock?"

"We'll be there. And, Mr. Kaplan—"

"Call me Ben."

"Ben . . . *thanks!*"

C.C. threw down the phone and let out a shriek of pure ecstasy. Throwing her arms in the air she jumped up and down, crying, "We did it! We did it! We did it!" Finally, when she was too exhausted to move, she collapsed on the floor and just grinned.

But it was impossible to sit still. Robin was at the

library and Gail and Annette were in school, but there had to be someone else she could tell. Ian! She ran downstairs and pounded on the door of the *Rock Rag* offices, but no one was there. Hurrying back upstairs she picked up the phone, ready to call someone, anyone. But who? Her mother? No, every phone conversation they'd had since C.C. moved out had ended in a fight. Daddy? Well, sure, why not? Two months ago he'd told her she had to make it on her own, and now, by God, she had!

She was just about to dial his office when Robin walked through the door. "Oh, man," she said wearily, "what a morning. Jennings handed our term papers back and I got a C. Can you believe it? I mean, I worked my rear end off on that thing and . . ." She paused and peered at her roommate. "C.C., you look kind of weird. You haven't been hitting the tequila again, have you?"

C.C. just laughed. "You got a phone call while you were out, dear roommate. Someone named, uh . . . Ben Kaplan, I think he said his name was. Ever hear of him?"

"Ben Kaplan! Omigod! What did he say?"

C.C. smiled mysteriously. "Oh, not much. Just that he wants us to come to his office tomorrow . . . to discuss a recording contract."

"Whooo!" Robin threw down her books and rushed into C.C.'s arms. Together they danced around the living room, shrieking and giggling and grinning from ear to ear. Then, suddenly, Robin stopped and ran to the window. Throwing it open she leaned out and cried triumphantly, "Look out, world! Here comes Overnight Sensation!"

"We're going to be famous!" C.C. screamed over her shoulder. "Do you hear me? Famous!"

An elderly lady looked up in alarm, and a bearded

man sitting on the steps of the Newcomers Motorcycle Club shook his head and called, "Sure, kids. And I'm the Prince of Wales."

"Take a good look now, buddy," Robin yelled back, "because pretty soon you'll be seeing our pictures on a album cover!"

C.C. threw her arm over Robin's shoulder and shouted so loud she scared the pigeons off the window-sills. "We're going to be a rock 'n' roll stars!"

Robin called Annette and Gail that afternoon, and at eleven o'clock the next morning they all met outside Backstage Records' Broadway office. "I can't believe this is really happening!" Annette said breathlessly. "I'm so excited!"

"This is the first time I ever skipped school," Gail confided. "Do you think it'll be okay?"

"Relax," C.C. told her. "When your teachers find out you're putting out an album, they'll be too busy asking for your autograph to care about anything else."

The girls walked inside the building and took the elevator up to the Backstage Records' office. Miss Prist was sitting behind the reception desk, reading the latest issue of *Cosmo*. When she saw Robin, she sighed dramatically and said, "Listen, young lady, how many times do I have to tell you? Mr. Kaplan is busy. If and when he gets around to listening to your tape, he'll get back to you. Understand?"

Robin rested her hands on the desk and leaned forward until Miss Prist's face was only inches away. "For your information, Mr. Kaplan has already listened to our tape. We're here to discuss a contract." She smiled grimly. "And yes, we *do* have an appointment."

"Oh . . . well, I see." Flustered, she picked up the

phone. "Mr. Kaplan, Robin Quinn and her band are here. She—oh. Yes, sir. Of course, sir. Right away." Pursing her lips she lowered the receiver and muttered, "Through the door and down the hall. Second office on your right. Mr. Kaplan's expecting you."

"Thanks, Prist." Robin chuckled. "Keep up the good work."

Giggling, the girls followed Robin to Ben Kaplan's office. He met them at the door, a short, pudgy man with shoulder-length blond hair and a drooping mustache. Sort of the aging hippie type, Robin thought, surveying his faded jeans and rumpled white shirt. He smiled at her and his eyes twinkled like a counterculture Santa Claus. "Hi, girls. I'm Ben Kaplan. Call me Ben, please. You must be Robin . . . Gail . . . Annette. And you're C.C. We spoke yesterday on the phone. Come on in and make yourself comfortable."

Ben sat behind his desk and the girls arranged themselves on the cushioned chairs. The walls were decorated with framed album covers and gold records, and there were two Grammy Awards on his desk. "So," he began, leaning back in his chair, "I thought you were bringing your manager."

"We don't have one," Robin said. "Since we split from Reg Barthwaite we've been on our own."

Ben nodded. "That's cool, but you're definitely going to want a lawyer to help you negotiate the contract. You'll probably want to hire a manager sooner or later too. Rock 'n' roll can get pretty crazy sometimes. It helps to have someone to handle the business end of things."

Negotiate the contract. The words made Robin feel a little lightheaded. "So you . . . you really want to sign us?" she asked, hardly daring to believe it was true.

Ben chuckled. "I certainly do. I think you girls have

everything it takes to be stars. All you need is a record company that's committed to promoting you. And that's Backstage Records." He sat forward and folded his hands on the desk. "Now let me explain what's going to happen. First of all, you go find yourself a good lawyer and tell him to call me. The two of us will negotiate a contract, and when you're satisfied, we'll all sign. Okay?"

The girls nodded.

"Now let me give you my thoughts on the band," Ben continued. "All-girl bands are still pretty unusual, but the novelty's wearing off. The record business already has two female bands that have made their mark with a cute appearance and bouncy, sixties-influenced music—the Go-Go's and Bangles. Well, that's fine, but in my opinion, the public's really for something new."

"Like us?" Robin asked hopefully.

Ben smiled. "Exactly. Now, don't get me wrong, you girls are cute. But you're a lot more than that. Your music is more hard-rocking, more intense, than what people expect from an all-girl group. What I'm saying is this: I think we can make Overnight Sensation the first all-girl band to really be taken seriously. It's not going to be easy—after all, you're only teenagers—but if we put out a strong first album backed with the right kind of publicity campaign—you know, comparing you to bands like U2 and the Pretenders instead of Bangles and the Go-Go's—I think we've got a chance." He put his elbows on the desk and leaned forward. "Well, what do you think?"

"I think it sounds great!" Robin enthused.

"It's sure a lot better than what Reg had in mind," Annette said. Gail and C.C. nodded eagerly.

"Good." He stood up and shook each girl's hand. "Now hurry up get yourselves a lawyer. The sooner we get this contract b.s. out of the way, the sooner we can start on the important stuff—like records, videos, interviews—"

"*Stardom!*" C.C. chimed in.

"Yeah." Ben grinned, ushering them out the door. "That too."

As soon as they left Backstage Records, C.C. called her father and told him they needed a lawyer. Two days later the band had hired Thomas J. Donleavy, Esquire, to represent them. Between meetings with Mr. Donleavy life went on more or less as usual. C.C. started a waitressing job at a Lower East Side deli. She was still dating so much that when Kurt got back from England and started phoning she was never home. Robin took his messages but C.C. refused to call back, and after a week he stopped trying.

Gail was busy convincing her parents that signing a contract with Backstage Records wouldn't keep her from attending Juilliard in the fall. She had no idea whether it was true or not, but she certainly wasn't going to worry about that now. The rest of her time was spent at the All-City Club, where Flip was introducing her to everyone as "my girlfriend, the rock star."

Meanwhile, the girls were practicing together again and Robin was working on some new songs, including one using Annette's lyrics. Since they'd signed the contract, Ian never seemed to be around much, but Robin was too busy to pay much attention. Besides, she reminded herself, they'd be spending lots of time together once Overnight Sensation went into the studio to cut their first album.

Negotiations took almost a month. When the contracts were finally signed, Overnight Sensation got a one-hundred-thousand-dollar advance, eighty thousand of which was earmarked to produce the first album. With the remaining twenty thousand dollars they still had to pay off the lawyer and buy new equipment. In the end they were left with four thousand dollars, which they split four ways. Not exactly big bucks, but it was a start.

The next step was to meet their new producer. Backstage Records wanted someone with a track record, so they hired Martin Jones. Jones was known for his work with sixties girl groups like the Shantells and the Ingenues, as well as some current middle-of-the-road bands like Kid Brother, the Stanford Robinson Band, and Hurly Burly.

"But, Ben," Robin protested as he led the girls down the hallway to his office. "Martin Jones is all wrong for our band. He's into violins and four-part harmonies, not high-powered rock 'n' roll. We need someone who's on our wavelength. Like that guy who produces R.E.M., or the one who did the first Big Country album, what's his name—?"

"Steve Lillywhite. Look," Ben whispered, "I'm on your side, but the higher-ups said no. They don't want to shell out the money for a big name like Lillywhite."

"But, Ben—" Gail began.

"Shh. Jones is waiting in my office right now."

Ben herded the girls around the corner and Martin Jones rose to meet them. He was a small, middle-aged man with black, wispy hair and pasty white skin. His eyes were obscured by mirrored sunglasses and his handshake was moist and limp. After the introductions everyone sat down.

"I heard your demo," Jones said, "and let me tell you, I'm really excited about this record. I hear a sort of Phil Spector wall-of-sound with a little techno-pop mixed in."

"But we've got our own sound," Annette interrupted. "We don't want to change it."

"Neither do I. All we're going to do is punch it up a little. Some horn charts, a drum machine, synthesizers . . ."

"Uh, that reminds me," Robin said, "—we promised the guy who produced our demo that he could play on our first album. His name is Ian Harkin and he's a really good synthesizer pla—"

"Out of the question," Jones said, shaking his head vigorously. "I've got my own sessions players and I don't use anyone else."

"But, Mr. Jones—"

"Let's not argue. I've had a lot of bad experiences with this sort of thing in the past. Making hit records is my job—a job I'm damn good at—and I do it my way or not at all."

"I like the second suggestion," C.C. muttered under her breath.

"Okay," Ben broke in quickly, "let me explain what Backstage Records has in mind. We'd like you to record a single first, and we'll release it along with a video while you're recording the rest of the album. With any luck we'll have a hit on our hands by the time the album comes out. Then we can release a second single and another video to really boost sales."

"Sounds reasonable," Jones said with a nod. He looked at the girls. "I've booked time at Brick House Studios for next Monday night." He stood up and smiled at Ben. "Got to go. I've got a recording session with Hurly Burly in half an hour."

As soon as Jones had left, Ben turned to the girls and held up his hands. "Now, I know what you're going to say. But let's just give it a chance, okay? Martin is a genius in the recording studio and I think once you hear what he can do, you're going to be pleasantly surprised."

"But what about—"

"Girls, look. My hands are tied. According to your contract we have the right to choose your producer. The head of the A&R Department picked Jones, and that's that."

With a heavy heart Robin led the girls out of Ben's office. Jones might be a good producer, she thought miserably, but he isn't right for Overnight Sensation. That's obvious.

But that wasn't all Robin was upset about. Ian had done the band a big favor by producing their demo tape for free. All he asked in return was to play on the girls' first album, and Robin had told him—no, *promised* him—it would happen. "Oh, Lord," she moaned as she dragged herself into the elevator, "what am I going to tell him now?"

‖‖‖‖‖‖‖‖‖‖‖‖‖‖‖ 14

I might as well get this over with fast, Robin told herself as she walked to Ian's apartment. The longer I wait, the crummier I'll feel.

Ian lived on East Ninth Street in a one-room basement apartment. Circling around the garbage cans that lined the pavement she walked up to his door and knocked. No answer. She knocked harder and Ian appeared at the door wearing nothing but a baby-blue terry-cloth robe. His curly hair was mussed and his eyes were only half open. Robin thought he looked absolutely adorable. "What are you doing here?" he asked hoarsely. "The sun isn't even up yet."

"Yes, it is. It's ten o'clock." Momentarily forgetting why she'd come, she reached up and tousled his hair. "You look cute."

Ian laughed and put his arms around her waist. "Well, as long as you're here, come on in. It's awfully lonely sleeping in that big old bed all by myself."

"I—I . . . Ian, I have to talk to you."

"What's wrong?" he asked, eyeing her closely. "Come on in and tell me."

Robin followed him into the tiny apartment. She'd been there so often she knew every inch by heart—the exposed brick walls lined with shelves of records and paperbacks, the comfy old purple sofa with its torn cushions, stacks of milk cartons he used to store his clothes in, an orange futon he kept rolled in the corner during the daytime and unrolled to sleep on at night. . . .

"Well?" Ian stepped over the futon and sat on the couch. Robin followed, her stomach churning.

"Ian," she began shakily, "we met our producer today. It's Martin Jones, that guy who produced all the Hurly Burly albums."

"What? Hurly Burly plays light rock, real laid-back stuff. I hope this Jones guy realizes you don't fit into that category."

"Yeah, me too. But anyhow, I told him we want you to play synthesizer on the album, and well, uh"—her voice dropped to a whisper—"he said no."

"Oh."

Robin glanced up at Ian, trying to gauge his reaction. His face was expressionless, but there was a pained look in his dark-brown eyes. "I told him we promised you," she said quickly, "but he said he never uses anybody but his own sessions players. I tried to explain to Ben, but—"

"Never mind, Robin. I don't want any favors. You made it on your own and I've got to do it that way too."

"But, Ian, you produced our demo and—"

"Look, none of that matters now, does it? You've got your career to think about. You can't afford to worry about me."

"But I do worry about you. I—"

"Don't bother, Robin. I may not be a big rock star like you, but I'm not doing so bad."

"Oh, Ian, I didn't mean it like that. It's just that I care about you and I want you to be happy."

"Sure, sure. Look, Robin, I'd like to keep talking, but I've got to get dressed. I'm going to Haverford to see my folks this weekend and my train leaves in less than an hour."

"Oh. You didn't tell me you were going away this weekend. I mean, is everything all right?"

"Of course everything's all right," he snapped. "Can't I even plan a visit to my parents without reporting to you first?" He stood up and started folding the sheets on his bed. With his back to her he muttered, "I'll see you later, okay?"

Forcing back tears Robin got up and walked to the door. "Good-bye, Ian," she said shakily. "Have a good weekend." When he didn't answer, she opened the door and left.

Out on the street the sun was shining and sparrows were chirping in the trees. A beautiful spring day, but to Robin the world seemed as cold and bleak as an Arctic blizzard. Wiping the tears from her eyes she turned her back on Ian's apartment and headed for home.

When Robin went down to the *Rock Rag* office on Monday, she found Eddie sitting in Ian's chair, editing one of Robin's reviews. "Uh, isn't that usually Ian's job?" she asked.

"Yeah," Eddie replied, "but he called me last night and told me to do it. He's out of town."

"Did he say how long he'll be gone?" Robin asked.

"Nope. But he said if he wasn't back by next week, I should take the articles to the typesetter and do the paste-up myself."

"Oh." Robin left the office burning with frustration. She wanted to talk to Ian, to put her arms around him and tell him she loved him. But until he came back to the city, there was nothing she could do about it. She'd just have to wait and hope that he was missing her as much as she was missing him.

That night the girls met Martin Jones at Brick House Studios. "This place is incredible!" Robin gasped as they walked in. "Wall-to-wall carpeting, air conditioning, the works!"

"Not to mention state-of-the-art thirty-two track equipment," Jones added.

"Look at this!" Annette called from the hallway. "Free video machines. And a refrigerator filled with drinks."

"Come on, kids." Jones chuckled. "You can play Pac-Man later. Right now we've got a record to make." The girls gathered around the mixing board. "Okay, to start off I want to play you what we've recorded so far."

"But we just got here," Gail said. "We haven't recorded anything yet."

"Not *you*," he explained. "The studio musicians. Ben told me he wants to release 'The Time of My Life' as the first single, so I had some guys come in last night and lay down a few tracks. Synthesizer, drum machines, horns, that sort of thing." He pushed some buttons and the tape started to roll. Suddenly the room was filled with music. It was "The Time of My Life"—everything minus the vocals.

"Hey!" cried Robin. "What gives? You recorded the entire thing without us!"

"Not at all," Jones replied. "I want Annette to add some drum fills over the drum machine, and Robin, we still need the rhythm guitar parts. And of course, you'll all be singing."

"What about me?" Gail demanded. "Don't I get to play at all?"

"Well, of course. It's just that on this particular song I thought it would be better to use someone with a little more experience. The bass line is so important in—"

"This is incredible!" Annette shouted. "First you tell us we can't use Ian. Now you don't even want to use *us!*"

Jones stopped the tape. "Girls, don't be ridiculous. Everybody uses studio musicians these days."

"Sure, one or two!" Robin retorted. "But not in place of the main band!"

"Now, now," he answered, wagging his finger, "we mustn't let our egos get in the way of the music. Remember, it's the song that counts, not—"

"That's it!" Robin shouted, vehemently shaking her head. "I've had it! I can't make a record like this. No way!"

"Now, now," Jones scolded, "I think you'd better get yourself under control."

But Robin was too angry to stop now. "You talk about ego," she cried, "but you're the one with the problem. You're so into yourself that you don't even care about the band you're supposed to be producing. Well, this is *our* record—Overnight Sensation—and we don't need you or any other hotshot producer to tell us how we're supposed to sound."

Jones eyed her coldly. "You won't get very far in this business with that attitude, young lady."

"Oh, yeah? Just watch us. Come on, girls. Let's get out of here!" Robin turned on her heel and stalked out of the studio. C.C., Annette, and Gail hesitated a second, then hurried after her.

"Hey, wait up!" C.C. called.

Robin was heading off down the hallway, but slowed down to let the girls catch up with her. "Well, I guess you told him." Annette chuckled, patting her on the back.

"What do we do now?" C.C. asked.

"Who knows?" Robin answered bitterly. "Jones is probably calling Ben Kaplan right now to tell him what a bunch of temperamental egomaniacs we are."

"Maybe we could talk Backstage into letting Ian produce us," Gail suggested. "After all, he did such a great job on our demo."

"But Backstage wouldn't even let him play on the single," Annette said. "What makes you think they'd ever agree to let him produce?"

"That was Jones who said that," C.C. reminded them, "not Ben."

Robin's mind was racing. Could they really convince Backstage Records to let Ian produce their first single? Even if they did, there was no guarantee that Ian would do it. Most likely he'd think Robin was just using her influence to help him out. Well, then, she thought with determination, I'll just have to convince him it's not true. But first I have to talk to Ben. . . .

"I've got an idea how we might be able to convince Backstage," she told the girls. "See, we'll make a deal with them. All they gotta do is let us record the song with Ian producing. In return we guarantee we'll come up with something better than Martin Jones could do, and at half the cost. If they like the results, they can release the song as our first single. If they don't—and here's the clincher—we promise we'll go back in the studio with Jones and finish up "The Time of My Life" exactly the way he wants it to be done." She shrugged. "Well, whaddaya think?"

"If we blow this, we're in deep trouble," C.C. warned.

"We're already in deep trouble," Annette reminded her. "A little bit more won't make any difference."

"Right," agreed Gail. "And if Robin's plan works . . ."

". . . we'll be showing Martin Jones and Ben Kaplan and everybody else at Backstage Records they can't push Overnight Sensation around!" Annette finished.

"Then let's do it!" Robin cried, pointing the way. The girls left Brick House Studios and hurried up the street toward Broadway. "Backstage Records, here we come!"

||||||||||||||||||||||| **15**

It took a lot of fast talking, but eventually the girls convinced Ben it was time to try things their way. He, in turn, convinced Backstage Records—with a few added conditions. For one thing, Ian had to use Howard Beatty as his engineer. Beatty was a seasoned engineer/producer and the owner of Brick House Studios, and Backstage figured things couldn't go too far wrong with him looking over Ian's shoulder. Second, the girls had exactly one week to come up with the tape. And third, if they went over budget, the band would make up the difference out of their own pockets. It was a hard bargain, but when they considered the alternative—adding vocals to Martin Jones's arrangement of "The Time of My Life"—they decided it was worth it.

Now the only problem was Ian. He was still in Haverford, and no one—not Eddie, not even the other guys in Naming of Parts—knew when he was coming back. The only solution, Robin realized, was to call him at his parents' house. That evening she dialed information and was told there were three Harkins in Haverford. The first person she called had never heard of Ian. The second was an old woman who said she was Ian's grandmother. "Who's this?" she demanded. "Ian's girlfriend?"

Taken aback, Robin stammered, "Well, I—I think so. I mean, I used to be. That is, I want to be, but, uh . . ."

"You sound a little confused, young lady. But let me give you a word of advice. If you're in love with my grandson, you'd better let him know it, and fast. He's been moping around his parents' house, talking a lot of nonsense about moving back home and going to business school." She snorted indignantly. "Rubbish. *Rubbish,* I say! Ian is a musician. He'd be absolutely miserable in the business world. Why, just yesterday I told him—"

"Excuse me, Mrs. Harkin, but uh, I think I better call Ian right now."

"You do that. And if you think of it, tell him I won't be needing that ride to Philadelphia tomorrow. One of the woman in my bridge club is driving in and she offered to take me. And that reminds me, if you talk to Ian's mother . . ."

Robin felt like screaming, but she heard Mrs. Harkin out and ended the conversation as politely as she could. Then, with trembling fingers, she dialed the Harkins' number. "Hello?" A woman's voice.

"Is Ian there?"

"Just a moment, please."

Robin chewed her lower lip and tried to come up with the perfect opening line. *Hey Ian, guess who?* No, too dumb. *Hi Ian. Filled out your business school applications yet?* No, too snide. *Hello Ian, I—*

"Hello?"

At the sound of Ian's voice, Robin's stomach turned to Jell-O. "I-Ian," she croaked.

"Robin? Is that you?"

"Yes." For some reason she felt like crying, and to cover up she blurted out the first thing that came into her mind. "Your grandmother doesn't need that ride to Philadelphia after all."

"Huh? What are you talking about?"

"Oh, brother," Robin moaned, running her hand over her face. "Uh, maybe I better start from the beginning." She took a deep breath and started talking. Five minutes later she'd told Ian everything that had happened since he'd left the city, from Overnight Sensation's fight with Martin Jones right through to the phone conversation she'd just had with Ian's grandmother. "So, Ian," she concluded, "we really want you to produce the single. It would mean so much to us."

There was a long moment of silence. "I don't know, Robin," Ian said finally. "Maybe it's just male pride or something, but I don't like the idea of you doing me favors just becau—"

"Ian," Robin moaned in exasperation, "it's *you* who'd be doing *me* the favor. I mean, if you don't get back here and help us out, Backstage Records is going to turn us into the Martin Jones Barbershop Quartet."

Ian chuckled, then paused and sighed deeply. "Okay, okay. But look, Robin, I'm going through a tough period right now. I'm feeling kind of uncertain about my music, about what I want to do with my life, about . . . well, practically everything. So, uh, as far as you and I are concerned, I think we'd better cool it for a while."

"But, Ian, I don't understand. If you're having problems, I want to help you work them out. I mean, that's what love is all about, isn't it?"

Love. It was the first time the word had ever been spoken between them. *I care about you,* or *I like you,* or *You're special,* sure, but never *I love you.* Well, it's true, Robin thought, I do love him. But did Ian feel the same? She held her breath and waited for his response.

"First things first," Ian said softly. "Right now I just want to concentrate on producing a hit single for Overnight Sensation. When that's over . . . well, I don't know. I guess I'll just have to wait and see how I feel."

"Oh," she muttered, trying to hide the hurt and disappointment that threatened to overwhelm her. She swallowed hard, holding back the tears, and said, "Ben booked time for us at Brick House Studios tomorrow night at eight. D-do you think you can get back that soon?"

"Yeah, I guess so. I'll meet you there. Bye."

"Good-bye." Hanging up the phone Robin dropped down on the red velvet sofa and burst into tears.

When Ian showed up outside Brick House Studios the next night he was all enthusiasm and smiles. "Okay, gang," he said, pulling them around him like a football coach before a big game, "we're going to handle this just like we did at Ground Sound. I'll record you live, then we'll overdub vocals, synthesizers, stuff like that. Jerry, the sax player from my band, is coming by later tonight to add some of his licks too." He smiled and patted them on the back. "Now, let's go in there and show Backstage Records we know how to rock!"

Robin, who had spent most of last night lying awake crying, glared at him and wondered how he could look so cheerful. I wrote that song about us, she thought miserably, but said nothing.

Robin hadn't told the others about her problems with Ian, and none of them seemed to notice the circles under her eyes or the pained expression on her face. "Great!" Gail said eagerly.

"Let's do it!" C.C. agreed.

While the girls set up their equipment, Ian introduced himself to Howard Beatty and looked around the studio. Robin watched him until she caught his eye, but when she smiled, he looked away.

After Beatty had run a sound check, Ian joined him in the control booth. From there he could see the band through a large plate-glass window and talk to them through an intercom. "Okay, rock stars," he said encouragingly, "we're ready to record. Now, don't forget, I want you to leave out the background vocals this time around. We'll overdub them later, just like we did at Ground Sound." The girls nodded. "This is 'The Time of My Life,' take one," he said clearly. "Count it off, Robin."

Robin stepped up to her microphone. "One, two,

three—" The band came in on four and C.C. started to sing.

*"Clouds as soft as angels' hair,
Don't tell me 'bout heaven 'cause I've been there.
When we walk together I look up at the sky,
It feels so right I can almost fly."*

Robin strummed her guitar and thought back to the night she'd written those words. It was the time Ian had invited her to the townhouse to hear Naming of Parts. Between sets—when they'd gone out to the diner for potato pancakes—that was the first time they'd ever walked side by side. I was so happy that night, Robin thought wistfully. I remember looking up at the clouds and thinking, *This feels so right. . . .*

Overcome by the memory she closed her eyes and sang the next line,

*"I take a breath, I take a step,
You take control, forget the rest—"*

"Hold it! Hold it!" Robin opened her eyes and looked around. The band had stopped playing and Ian was glaring at her from inside the control booth. "I said no backing vocals, remember?"

"Oh, sorry," Robin muttered, blushing with embarrassment.

"Okay, let's try it again. 'The Time of My Life,' take two."

Robin counted it off again and the band started playing. Concentrate, she told herself. Don't think about anything except the song. She stared at her guitar and strummed intently. But her mind kept returning to Ian. She loved the way he looked tonight. His faded black jeans hugged his hips and his red-and-black-striped shirt hung open at the neck, exposing a few curly brown chest hairs. Maybe he thinks I look good, too, she thought hopefully. In fact, maybe he's looking at me right now.

Robin glanced up and accidentally hit the wrong chord. Flustered, she tried to deaden the strings with the palm of her hand but succeeded only in dropping her pick on the floor.

"Hold it!" Ian called through the intercom.

"Now what?" C.C. asked irritably.

"It was my fault," Robin admitted. "I played the wrong chord." She looked at Ian, but he turned his gaze on the others.

"Come on gang," he said patiently, "let's try to relax. This studio is no different from Ground Sound. Just play the song exactly the way you did there and everything will be fine." He smiled reassuringly. " 'The Time of My Life,' take three. Now, come on, let's rock!"

Robin felt tense and irritable. Why is he treating me like this? she brooded. I can't help it if Overnight Sensation has a record contract and Naming of Parts doesn't. Maybe if they played some regular rock 'n' roll instead of that weird avant-garde stuff, they'd get somewhere. Here, Ian, she thought angrily. You wanna know what rock fans really like? Dig this!

She counted off the song and tore into a burning guitar solo. Startled, Gail played a wrong note and Annette lost the beat.

"Stop!" Ian shouted. "Cut! Cut! Robin, what the hell do you think you're doing? You aren't supposed to play a guitar solo there!"

"Oh, yeah?" she countered, too upset to care what she was doing. "Just watch me!" Looking him straight in the eye she whipped off a searing blues lick.

Ian stormed out of the control booth and grabbed Robin by the arm. "I want to talk to you. *Alone.*" Unplugging her guitar he half led, half dragged her across the room. Annette, Gail, and C.C. stared after them in bewilderment. "Take five!" he called over his shoulder as he pulled her out the door and kicked it shut.

Out in the hallway Ian dropped Robin's arm and turned to face her. "Okay, what's the big idea? You know there isn't supposed to be a guitar solo there."

"Of course I know," Robin retorted. "It's my song. I wrote it about you and me."

"You and me?" he repeated, momentarily brought up short. Robin nodded. "Okay," he continued, resuming his angry expression, "if you know the song so well, why are you making all those stupid mistakes?"

"Stupid mistakes? Look, Ian," she said bitterly, "the only stupid mistake I made was getting involved with you. But that's over now. You've made that clear enough." A sob rose in her throat and she turned away. "I guess I'm just having a little trouble getting used to the idea."

"Robin . . ." He reached out to touch her arm, but she pulled away. "Please don't cry. I know I'm acting like an idiot. It's just . . . well, I don't know. I guess I'm just jealous. I never thought you'd get a record deal this fast. Naming of Parts has sent out three demos and we still haven't had an offer."

"But I can't help that." Robin sniffled. "We're just more commercial, that's all. Besides, if it wasn't for your help, we never would have made it. You picked the songs, you arranged them, produced them—"

"I know, and that's part of what's bugging me. I never wanted to be a producer. I'm a musician—a songwriter, just like you. But here I am, producing your first single. It would be so easy to just forget about Naming of Parts and stick with that."

"Well, why not?" she asked, turning to face him. "If

Backstage Records likes this single, I'll bet they'll let you produce the whole album."

"It's tempting Robin, but I don't know. I want to make it to the top on my own, not riding on your coattails." He looked away. "Maybe I should just get out of music altogether. I could move back to Haverford, go to school—"

"Rubbish! That's what your grandmother said and she's right. You're a musician. You'd hate doing anything else."

Ian smiled. "I suppose so. But I've got to do it on my own terms." He gazed into her eyes and sighed. "I'm sorry I've been acting so crazy. I just thought maybe if I stopped seeing you for a while everything would fall into place. But I was wrong. I was miserable in Haverford. All I could think about was how much I missed you."

"Really?" she asked, hardly daring to believe it.

"Are you kidding? I'm a mess without you. I can't eat, can't sleep . . ." He put his arms around her and pulled her close. "I love you, Robin. I really do."

Robin started crying again, but this time they were tears of joy. "Oh, Ian," she said joyfully, "I love you too."

Smiling, he kissed the tears from her cheeks, then moved down until his lips were touching hers. "Robin . . ."

Suddenly the door to the studio flew open and Howard Beatty stuck his head out. "Hey, you two, time is money. You can work out your lovelife later. Right now we got a record to make."

"Oh, uh, sorry, Mr. Beatty," Ian muttered. "We'll be right in." He turned to Robin and said seriously, "Look, I have to be honest with you. I'm still pretty confused about things, and as you've probably noticed by now, confusion makes me kind of nuts. What I mean is, I really want us to stay together, but I can't guarantee it's going to be smooth sailing all the way."

"Hey," Robin said with a shrug, "I think I can handle it. I mean, as long as we keep loving each other, everything else is bound to work out eventually."

"Yeah." Ian nodded. "I guess you're right." He put his arm around her shoulder and gave her a squeeze. "Okay, rock star, are you ready to go back in there and lay down some hot tracks?"

"You bet. Like I wrote in the song—" She threw her arm around Ian's waist and they walked back into the studio, singing together,

> *"This time I know what I'm after,*
> *This time I'm doing it right.*
> *No tears, just love and laughter,*
> *This time I'm having the time of my life."*

16

Ben led the girls to the end of the hall and threw open the door marked A&R DEPARTMENT STAFF ROOM. Inside there were at least fifteen people, all sitting around a long table, smoking, drinking coffee, and talking. "Okay, folks," Ben announced loudly, herding the girls through the door, "here they are!" Instantly the room fell silent and all heads turned to stare at the girls. "I'd like you all to meet Robin, Annette, C.C., and Gail," he said. "Overnight Sensation!"

The girls just stood there, grinning self-consciously, until Ben motioned to four chairs at the end of the table. "I've got the tape right here," he said as they sat down. He walked to the side wall and pulled open a door, revealing a reel-to-reel tape-deck. "Let's see how it sounds." He set up the tape, pushed a few buttons, and suddenly the room was filled with the opening bars of "The Time of My Life."

"Clouds as soft as angels' hair," C.C. sang on the tape. "Don't tell me 'bout heaven 'cause I've been there."

Ian's synthesizer lines interwove with C.C.'s vocals and the saxophone squawked in funky counterpoint to Annette's drums and Gail's bass. After the first chorus a hot guitar lick propelled the song on to the next verse.

By the time the song moved into the second chorus, a few people were tapping their fingers on the table. A bearded man at the far end of the room was nodding his head in time with the beat. "Bernstein," Ben whispered. "Head of A&R." The girls looked at each other and smiled hopefully.

"No tears, just love and laughter," the girls were singing on the tape. "This time I'm having the time of my life."

The song ended and the tape flapped against the empty reel. "I like it," Ben said heartily, getting up to turn off the recorder.

"Good beat," a woman in a purple blouse added. "Definitely danceable."

"Strong production work," the Bernstein said. "That kid—what's his name—?"

"Ian," Robin piped up. "Ian Harkin."

"Yeah. He did a real good job." Bernstein sipped his coffee and stared off into space. "Know what?" he said finally. Everyone at the table leaned in a little closer, waiting to hear Bernstein's pronouncement. He smiled broadly. "I think we've got a hit on our hands."

The girls leapt out of their seats and hugged each other. "Thank you, Mr. Bernstein!" Robin cried gratefully.

"Thank you, *everyone!*" added Annette.

"We won't let you down," Gail assured them.

"Okay, kids," Ben broke in, herding them out the door, "you can celebrate later. Right now I want to tell you about the person who's going to direct your video. Her name is Lisa Hooper and she won an MTV Video Award last year for her video of the title tune to the movie *Break-dancin'.*"

"I saw that," Robin said. "It was great!"

Ben nodded. "I think you'll all get along just fine. At least I hope so. I don't want you walking out on her like you did on Martin Jones." He held up a warning finger. "You got away with that once, but don't press your luck. You know what I'm saying, kids?"

"Yes, sir, Mr. Kaplan, sir," C.C. said, throwing him a salute.

Ben laughed and led the girls into his office. "Lisa's got a great idea for you girls. She's been checking out the public art around Manhattan—you know, all those murals on the sides of buildings and the graffiti on the subways. She wants to shoot you performing the song in front of dozens of different murals, then edit them together to create a sort of collage effect. What do you think?"

"Sounds cool," C.C. said. The others nodded agreement.

"And how about some dancing?" Robin asked. "Videos always have that."

"I've got a suggestion," Gail said eagerly. "We could use Flip and his crew." She turned to Ben.

"They're called the Fresh Body Rockers and they're really good break-dancers."

"Sounds good. And you can learn some steps to do along with them."

"You want us to dance?" Annette asked skeptically.

"But I'm such a klutz," Robin moaned.

Ben smiled. "I'm sure you can handle it. There's going to be some boy-girl stuff too. Maybe some shots of you walking around the city with your boyfriends."

"We can use Flip and Ian," Gail suggested.

"They're our real boyfriends," Robin explained to Ben.

"How about you two?" he asked, turning to Annette and C.C. "Do you have boyfriends too?"

"Not me," Annette said, shaking her head.

Robin looked at C.C. "Maybe Kurt would like to be in the video."

"Forget it!" C.C. snapped. "It's all over between Kurt and me." She looked down at the floor. So why can't I forget him? she wondered sadly. No matter how many boys I go out with, I still keep thinking about him. She sighed. Maybe I should call him. But no, she told herself quickly. I can have my pick of guys. I don't need Kurt.

"No problem," Ben was saying. "We can come up with a couple of actors to play your boyfriends. Now all we've got to do is get you girls back in the studio to cut the flip side of the single." He leaned back in his chair and smiled broadly. "If it's anywhere as good as 'The Time of My Life,' who knows? We may have *two* hits on our hands!"

The girls spent the first half of May getting ready for the video. After scouting locations around the city Lisa Hooper put together a storyboard—a shot-by-shot outline of what the video was going to look like.

Rehearsals came next. Lisa booked time in a downtown dance studio, and with the help of the Fresh Body Rockers, she choreographed a few simple breakdancing moves for the girls to do together. After they had the dance moves down, they worked on the love scenes—shots of the girls and their boyfriends walking arm and arm by the river, eating lunch together at a sidewalk café, and kissing in the park.

Finally, Lisa met with everyone to discuss what clothes they should wear. Flip and his crew decided on matching black sweatsuits, red baseball caps, and red Pro-Keds. The girls were allowed to put together their own outfits. Lisa's only advice was that each girl wear something distinctive, something that would exemplify the rock 'n' roll image she wanted to project to the world. The boyfriends—Flip, Ian, and the two actors Lisa had hired to play opposite C.C. and Annette—were instructed to dress in styles that would complement the girls' clothing.

The taping was scheduled for six A.M. on a sunny spring morning. Robin was ready to go by five-thirty, but C.C. was still in bed with the pillow over her head. "Better get up," Robin warned, checking out her baggy forties-style pants, black suspenders, and rainbow-striped shirt in the mirror. "Lisa said she wants to start filming before the streets get too crowded."

"Yeah, yeah. I know. You go ahead. I'll be up in a minute."

"Okay." Robin pulled a black newsboy's-cap over her curly brown hair. "Just make sure you don't fall back asleep."

C.C. waited until she'd heard the front door close; then, rubbing the sleep from her eyes, she reached under her mattress and pulled out a bottle of brandy. Throwing back her head she put the bottle to her lips and let the burning liquid slide down her throat.

C.C., she asked herself, what are you doing? It's crazy to be gulping down brandy at five-thirty in the morning.

But how else could she face the taping? It had been tough enough at the rehearsals, watching Robin and Gail run through the love scenes with Ian and Flip while she had to pretend with Sebastian, the actor who had been hired to play her boyfriend. Not that Sebastian wasn't handsome. Wavy blond hair, big blue eyes, a great build—in short, a hunk. But he wasn't Kurt, and, as far as C.C. was concerned, that was all that mattered.

C.C. reached up and touched the heart-shaped pendant that hung around her neck. She hadn't taken it off since the night Kurt gave it to her. Oh, Kurt, she thought sadly, maybe I was wrong to tell you I wanted us to date other people while you were away. Maybe if I'd trusted you a little more, we'd be together right now.

Taking another swig of brandy she dragged herself out of bed and threw on the clothes she'd selected to wear in the video—a black leotard under a low-cut pink jersey with dropped shoulders, a white mini-skirt, and pink high-heeled boots. After fluffing up her hair with styling mousse and slapping on some makeup, she threw the brandy bottle into her purse and hurried out the door.

By the time C.C. made it to SoHo, the video crew was already setting up the equipment. Lisa Hooper, a small, deceptively meek-looking woman in khaki coveralls and work boots, was standing on the sidewalk, shouting orders to the men. "The girls are inside," she told C.C., pointing to a white van with the words LO-CATION VIDEO RECORDERS INC. on the side. "See what you can do about makeup. Robin looks pretty good, but Gail and Annette definitely need more. And come to think of it, you could use a little more liquid base to hide those rings under your eyes."

"Where's Ian and Flip and the others?"

"We're taping the love scenes later. I told the guys to show up around noon."

C.C. nodded glumly and left to join the others in the van.

The girls spent the morning lip-synching "The Time of My Life" in front of SoHo street murals, dancing in front of a grafitti-covered subway car, and pretending to play their instruments on a pigeon-infested rooftop. Whenever she had a chance, C.C. slipped the brandy bottle out of her purse and sneaked a sip. By the end of the morning she'd drunk enough to convince herself that she was looking forward to taping the love scenes with Sebastian. I can tell from the way he kissed me during rehearsals that he isn't just acting, she told herself. He likes me. I'm sure he does.

Around noon Lisa sent one of her assistants to buy lunch for everybody. When the food arrived, the girls went into the van to eat and wait for the next shot to be set up.

They were just polishing off a bag of Mrs. Fields Cookies when Lisa poked her head in the door and said, "We're all set up for the subway stairs scene."

Reluctantly C.C. followed the girls out of the van and down the nearest subway entrance, barely glancing at the guys as she went. The script called for the boys to be waiting on the sidewalk. The girls would then run up the stairs from the subway, meet the boys, and head off arm in arm down the street.

From the bottom of the stairs C.C. heard the music begin and Lisa yell, "Action!" Obediently she ran up the stairs, expecting to find Sebastian waiting for her. Instead she emerged into the sunlight and came face to face with . . . Kurt!

C.C.'s heart seemed to stop dead. Robin, Annette, and Gail were greeting their boyfriends and starting off down the street. C.C. knew she should do the same but she felt unable to move. Instead Kurt stepped forward and took her in his arms, kissed her, then grabbed her hand and led her down the street after the others.

"Cut!" Lisa called. "That was perfect. Now let's head over to Washington Square and set up for the scene in the park."

But C.C. wasn't listening. Stunned, she turned to Kurt. "W-what are you doing here?"

"You wouldn't answer my calls, so I decided I had to see you in person. I called Robin and she told me about the video. I decided right then and there that no one was going to play your boyfriend except me. Robin arranged things with Lisa Hooper and, well, here I am."

"Oh," she replied, trying to regain her composure. "Well, uh, how was your trip?"

Kurt looked at her searchingly. "Never mind that. Why didn't you come to meet me at the airport? Why haven't you returned any of my calls?"

"I've been busy," she answered carelessly. "We cut a single, and now we're doing this video, and after this we have to start on an album."

"I know. Robin told me." He sighed. "C.C., I need to talk to you. Let's sit down." He led her across the street to an ice cream shop with outdoor tables.

C.C. took a seat and reached for her purse. "You want some brandy?"

"No, thanks. C.C., about that girl in London. I want to explain. . . ."

"Hey, no problem. Like I said before you left, you're free to date anyone you want. We both are."

"Yeah, well I tried it, but it didn't work. In Paris I

went out with the daughter of one of my father's law friends. She was gorgeous, but she spent the whole evening telling me how much she hates Americans. Then in London I met Julie. We had fun together, but it was nothing serious. If I made it sound that way, it's only because I wanted to hurt you a little."

"But . . . but why?"

"Because you hurt me. When I told you I was going to Europe you sounded so eager to start dating other people. It was like you just couldn't wait to get rid of me. I figured you must have wanted to break up anyway, and my trip just gave you an easy way out."

"Oh, Kurt, it wasn't like that."

"Well, then, how was it?"

"I . . . well . . . oh, what does it matter?" She put her head in her hands and sighed wearily. "I hurt you, you hurt me. It's too late to change that now."

"Who says? I thought we were going to reevaluate things after I got back." He reached over and ran his hand across C.C.'s cheek. "Isn't that what you said?"

Kurt's touch left C.C. weak with pleasure. Could it really be that he was still interested in her? "Y-yes," she muttered. "That's what I said."

"Well, what do you think? Do you still care about me? Or have you found somebody new?"

C.C. felt confused and a little scared. If she put her heart on the line, what would happen? I've been hurt before, she reminded herself. I don't want it to happen again. She turned to Kurt, ready to tell him it was all over. But before she could speak he moved closer and kissed her gently on the lips. A rush of tingling warmth shot through her and she leaned back against the chair with her head spinning. "Kurt," she said breathlessly, "I never wanted to lose you. I was just scared."

"Scared of what?" he asked, reaching over to stroke her hair.

"Scared that you were going to break my heart. It was silly, I guess, but I've been hurt by men before. My father walked out, and Reg—"

"Reg? You mean that guy who used to manage C.C. and the Seniors? I didn't know you went out with him."

"I never told you. I was too embarrassed. I mean, he was just using me, but it took me a while to get wise."

"Hey, what happened between you and Reg has nothing to do with us. I'd never treat you like that. I love you."

"Still?" she asked incredulously. "Even after all the time we've been apart?"

"Of course. The question is, how do you feel about me?"

C.C. put her arms around Kurt and kissed him deeply. "Does that answer your question?" she asked with a mischievous smile.

"I think I'm getting the idea. But maybe you'd better tell me again." He closed his eyes and C.C. gave him another kiss. "Hmm," he murmured approvingly. "C.C., you have a real way with words."

"Why, thank you, Mr. Vandenburg." She giggled. "You're quite fluent yourself."

Kurt put his arm around her and she rested her head on his shoulder. "C.C.," he said, "we've got a lot of catching up to do. I want to tell you about my trip and about the art project I've been working on since I got back. And I want to hear about you . . . the band, your new apartment, everything." He sat up and took her hand. "How long do we have to tape today?"

"Lisa said we're not stopping until the sun goes down."

"Well, when we finish, I'm taking you out to dinner. Someplace really romantic with white tablecloths and candlelight and a spectacular view. After that we'll take one of those night cruises around Manhattan and kiss under the stars."

"Sounds wonderful," C.C. dreamily. "Just you and me and—"

"Hey, lovebirds!" C.C. looked up to see the white van pulling up to the sidewalk. Lisa grinned at them from the front seat. "I hate to spoil a romantic moment, but it just so happens we've got a video to make."

The back door of the van flew open and Robin, Annette, and Gail stuck their heads out. "Next stop, Washington Square Park," Robin called. "All aboard!"

Kurt laughed and stood up, but C.C. held back. "Hold on a sec." Pulling the brandy bottle out of her purse she turned and jogged into the ice cream shop. "Good-bye, booze," she whispered, lifting the lid of a plastic garbage can and dropping the bottle in. "I won't be needing you anymore." With a triumphant smile she replaced the lid and ran back to join Kurt and the others in the back of the van.

At the beginning of June the single—with "In My
Rainbow Room" on the flip side—started showing up
in the record stores. About a week later Ben called
Robin with some good news. Overnight Sensation's
video was premiering on *Friday Night Videos* next
weekend!

"We've gotta watch it together," Annette declared
when she heard the news.

"Maybe we could all go over to my parents' place,"
Robin suggested. "They have a color TV, and a VCR
too."

"I've got a better idea," C.C. told them. "Let's have
a party! We'll invite everybody over to our apartment
—our friends, our parents, the video crew, Ben Kaplan . . ."

"A celebration bash!" cried Annette. "With food
and music and dancing . . ."

"And Robin's folks can bring over their TV," Gail
added.

"All *right!*" C.C. shouted, raising her fist in a joyous
salute. "Let's *do* it!"

On Friday evening the girls got together to decorate
the apartment. Each girl was wearing the clothes she
had worn in the video. C.C. was in her black leotard
with her pink blouse and white miniskirt, complete

with dozens of necklaces and jangly bracelets. Robin was decked out in her rainbow-striped shirt and black pants, along with a black Indiana Jones–style hat she'd just picked up in a secondhand store. Annette— never one for dressing up—wore jeans, a sky-blue T-shirt, and her old black leather jacket. And Gail, once the most conservative dresser in the band, looked just right in white parachute pants and a white sleeve-less T-shirt with a purple bandana around her neck.

"Did I tell you I saw our single in the window of Tower Records?" Robin asked, climbing up the ladder to tape a red balloon above the window.

"Only about three hundred times." Annette chuckled. She was standing on the back of the red velvet sofa, hanging strands of multicolored crêpe paper from the ceiling.

"Well, it's exciting. Just a few months ago we didn't have enough money to record a demo tape, and now our single is in all the stores."

"We still don't have enough money," C.C. said with a pout. "I thought rock stars were rich. We can barely pay the rent."

Robin laughed scornfully. "We'd be doing okay if you hadn't spent your entire thousand-dollar advance on new clothes."

"Hey, we lead singers have to look good, you know?" She glanced over at Gail. "What time is it? I thought some people would have shown up by now."

Gail put down the bowl of potato chips she was carrying and looked at her watch. "It's only nine-thirty. No one's going to show up until ten at least."

"I know, I know. But I'm ready to party!" C.C. dropped the balloons and danced across the living room.

"I still can't believe this is happening," Annette said dreamily. *"Our* video, premiering tonight on *Friday*

Night Videos. It's unreal!" She glanced over at Gail, who was munching a potato chip and staring mournfully out the window. "Hey, what's the matter with you? Aren't you excited?"

"Sure, it's not that. I was just thinking about tonight. Maybe I shouldn't have invited my family. I mean, my parents have never met Flip, and I just know they're going to hate him."

"Never?" Robin asked with amazement. "But what about all those nights you and Flip went out dancing together? What did you tell your folks?"

"I said I was practicing with the band. They don't like that, either, but at least they're resigned to the idea."

"So what's wrong with Flip?" Annette asked. "I mean, they can't complain he's the wrong color."

Gail laughed weakly. "No, but there's plenty of other things for them to disapprove of. The way he dresses, the way he talks, the fact that he dropped out of high school . . ."

"I didn't know that," Robin said.

"I didn't, either, until a couple of weeks ago. I'm trying to talk him into going back, but I don't think it's working. He's making too much money at breakdancing to care about school."

"Speaking of high school," Annette broke in, "it's only two weeks until graduation!" She jumped off the sofa and snapped her fingers. "Whoopie! As soon as I get that diploma it'll be good-bye Brooklyn, hello East Village!"

"You, too, right Gail?" C.C. asked.

Gail sighed and shook her head. "I'd love to move in with all of you, but how can I? I don't have any money. My thousand dollars is going toward my tuition at Juilliard."

"Forget Juilliard," C.C. told her. "You've got a rock 'n' roll career to think about."

"It's not that simple. I promised my parents. Besides, I really want to go. I love rock, but I miss the classical music I used to play."

The doorbell rang and C.C. went to answer it. A moment later she reappeared with Kurt. "Look out, ladies!" he announced with a grin. "The world's greatest party animal has just arrived!" Growling ominously, he pounced on C.C.

"Oh, you beast!" she giggled as he kissed her.

Ian showed up a minute later carrying a case of beer. "You think we can fit all these bottles into the fridge?"

"Don't worry," Robin told him. "There isn't any food in there. We're broke again, as usual."

"Just wait till 'The Time of My Life' hits the charts," he replied, stepping onto the bottom rung of the ladder to give her a kiss. "When those royalty checks start rolling in, you'll be on easy street."

The next guests to arrive were Robin's parents and her brother, Hank. While the girls finished putting up the balloons and streamers, Mr. Quinn set up the television and the VCR.

"Let there be music!" C.C. cried, stacking records on the turntable. She flipped a switch and the latest Culture Club album came blasting through the speakers.

By ten-thirty the living room was filling up with people—Flip and the rest of the Fresh Body Rockers, Lisa Hooper, Eddie from *Rock Rag,* the guys from Naming of Parts, even C.C.'s father and his girlfriend, Bonnie.

"Cathy, honey," Mr. Collins asked, looking around the room with an expression of barely concealed dismay, "is this where you live?"

"That's right," she answered. "Home sweet home."

Her father frowned. "I know I said I wouldn't give you any more money unless you went to college, but, um, maybe I went a bit too far. After all, I don't like to think of my daughter living in a slum." He reached into his pocket and pulled out his wallet.

C.C.'s first reaction was to grab the money, but then she stopped and thought it over. These last few months on her own had been kind of nice. No parents around to tell her what she could and couldn't do. And no handouts to make her feel guilty and indebted. With a determined shake of her head she thrust her hands in her pockets and said, "Thanks, Daddy, but no thanks. I don't need your money. I'm doing just fine on my own."

"But, Cathy—"

"If she doesn't want it, don't force it on her," Bonnie said quickly, shooting Mr. Collins a disapproving glance.

The doorbell rang and C.C. grabbed the opportunity to retreat. By now, the party was in full swing. A Michael Jackson album was on the stereo and Fresh Body Rockers were amazing everybody with their moves.

"Hey, everybody!" C.C. looked around to see Robin leading Ben Kaplan through the door. "I want you all to meet the guy who signed us to Backstage Records. Our hero, Ben Kaplan!"

The room cheered and Ben smiled modestly. "I thought you'd want to see this," he said, pulling a rolled-up sheet of paper from under his arm. "It's a publicity poster we're going to send to record stores. What do you think?"

Ben unfurled the poster and the girls gasped. It was a photograph of the band taken the day they made the video. They were performing on a SoHo rooftop in front of a huge mural of the *Mona Lisa.* Under the photo were the words OVERNIGHT SENSATION! NEW MUSIC FROM BACKSTAGE RECORDS AND TAPES.

"Wow!" Robin said with awe, "we look like real rock stars!"

Ben laughed. "You *are* real rock stars." He handed her the poster. "Come on, lets hang this up."

The doorbell rang again and Annette went down to answer it. She discovered her parents and Gail's parents eyeing each other uneasily. "Mom, Dad," she said, "these are Gail's parents, Mr. and Mrs. Harrison."

"Why, Annette," her mother said with amazement, "I didn't know your band was integrated!"

Mr. Harrison let out a contemptuous snort and Annette felt her cheeks grow hot with shame. "Come on in," she said, hurrying her parents up the stairs.

"Annette, hurry up!" C.C. cried as she came in the door. *"Friday Night Videos* is on!"

Gail was sitting on the sofa holding hands with Flip. When she saw her parents her stomach began to churn and she wondered wildly if she could hide behind the sofa before they noticed her.

"Gail!" Mrs. Harrison exclaimed. "There you are!"

Too late. "Mom, Dad," she said weakly, "this is Flip."

Flip jumped up and stuck out his hand and Mr. Harrison shook it. "Do you have a last name, Flip?" he asked sternly.

"Sure do. Actually, my name's Morris Boone, but folks call me Flip-Flop 'cause of my fresh breakin' moves."

"You mean break-dancing?" Mrs. Harrison asked uncertainly.

"You got it. My crew did some cool rockin' in Gail's video. And you know," he added, putting his arm around her shoulder, "this chick's turnin' into a pretty awesome breaker herself."

Mr. Harrison frowned and opened his mouth to respond, but suddenly someone cried, "Here it is! Here it is!" and everybody turned to look at the television.

"And now," the announcer was saying, "the world premiere of a video by a brand new group. Here's Overnight Sensation singing 'The Time of My Life.'"

The girls let out a squeal of delight as their faces filled the screen, lip-synching the song in front of the *Mona Lisa* mural. The next shot showed them singing and dancing inside a grafitti-covered subway train.

"That's my little girl!" Mrs. Giraldi cried, pointing at the television.

"You call this music?" Mr. Giraldi grumbled. "It sounds like a truck changing gears." He shook his head, but Annette noticed he never took his eyes off the screen.

The rest of the video showed the girls singing on rooftops, in vacant lots, in the middle of the street, and even on the deck of the Staten Island ferry. Between those shots were scenes of the girls dancing with the Fresh Body Rockers, strolling through Washington Square with their boyfriends, and spray painting graffiti on a bench in Tompkins Square Park.

Then suddenly it was over and everyone broke into enthusiastic applause. "Hey, we didn't look half bad!" Annette exclaimed.

C.C. was frowning. "I don't know. My hair was a mess. And why didn't someone tell me my left earring had fallen off?"

"Gimme a break!" laughed Robin, punching her affectionately. "You looked terrific, as usual."

"Next week the video will start airing on MTV," Ben told them. "Oh, and by the way, I just remembered, we've booked three weeks of studio time starting next week. We want to get this album recorded by the end of the month so you can start touring as soon as possible."

"Touring?" Annette repeated blankly. "You mean like playing in clubs?"

"Clubs, concert halls, anyplace you can get a booking."

"In the city," Gail asked, "right?"

"Sure, for starters. Then New Jersey, Connecticut, up through New England—"

"But Annette's going to college," Mrs. Giraldi broke in. "She won't have time to go on any trips."

Annette sighed. "Mom, I told you a thousand times, I'm not interested in college right now."

"Our daughter has already been accepted at Juilliard," Mr. Harrison said firmly.

"But it's only part time," Gail argued. "I can still perform with the band on weekends."

"Look," Ben said firmly, "if you don't get out there and push the product it's going to bomb. You girls should be happy that Backstage Records is willing to give you tour support money. Most companies won't do that these days, especially not for a new band."

"Uh, Ben," Ian said hesitantly, "about the album. Do you have a producer in mind?"

"Why, *you,* of course. You and Howard Beatty did such a good job on the single. Everyone in A&R was extremely impressed."

"Thanks but, uh, I don't know if I want to do it. You see, I'm really more of a musician than a producer. I've got my own band and—hey!"

Ian ducked as a champagne cork flew over his head. "A toast!" Kurt cried, lifting the overflowing champagne bottle over his head. "Bring on the glasses."

Robin ran to open a package of plastic cups and

C.C. gave Kurt a hug. "Perfect timing," she whispered. "Thanks."

"No problem. After all, this is supposed to be a celebration, not a business meeting." The girls handed out the cups and Kurt poured the champagne. "To Overnight Sensation!" he exclaimed. "And to my favorite rock stars—C.C., Robin, Gail, and Annette!"

"To Overnight Sensation!" everyone cried.

The girls raised their glasses in the air and grinned joyfully. It was amazing, Robin reflected, how just when they thought they had it made, a whole new batch of problems cropped up. Oh, well, there'd be plenty of time to work things out—starting tomorrow. She threw back her head and downed the entire glass of champagne in one bubbly gulp. Right now it was time to party!

FOR THE BEST IN PAPERBACKS, LOOK FOR THE

In every corner of the world, on every subject under the sun, Penguin represents quality and variety – the very best in publishing today.

For complete information about books available from Penguin – including Pelicans, Puffins, Peregrines and Penguin Classics – and how to order them, write to us at the appropriate address below. Please note that for copyright reasons the selection of books varies from country to country.

In the United Kingdom: For a complete list of books available from Penguin in the U.K., please write to *Dept E.P., Penguin Books Ltd, Harmondsworth, Middlesex, UB7 0DA*

In the United States: For a complete list of books available from Penguin in the U.S., please write to *Dept BA, Penguin, 299 Murray Hill Parkway, East Rutherford, New Jersey 07073*

In Canada: For a complete list of books available from Penguin in Canada, please write to *Penguin Books Canada Ltd, 2801 John Street, Markham, Ontario L3R 1B4*

In Australia: For a complete list of books available from Penguin in Australia, please write to the *Marketing Department, Penguin Books Australia Ltd, P.O. Box 257, Ringwood, Victoria 3134*

In New Zealand: For a complete list of books available from Penguin in New Zealand, please write to the *Marketing Department, Penguin Books (NZ) Ltd, Private Bag, Takapuna, Auckland 9*

In India: For a complete list of books available from Penguin, please write to *Penguin Overseas Ltd, 706 Eros Apartments, 56 Nehru Place, New Delhi, 110019*

In Holland: For a complete list of books available from Penguin in Holland, please write to *Penguin Books Nederland B.V., Postbus 195, NL–1380AD Weesp, Netherlands*

In Germany: For a complete list of books available from Penguin, please write to *Penguin Books Ltd, Friedrichstrasse 10 – 12, D–6000 Frankfurt Main 1, Federal Republic of Germany*

In Spain: For a complete list of books available from Penguin in Spain, please write to *Longman Penguin España, Calle San Nicolas 15, E–28013 Madrid, Spain*